FROM USA TODAY BESTSELLING AUTHOR
ERIN BEDFORD

More From The Author

The Underground Series
Chasing Rabbits
Chasing Cats
Chasing Princes
Chasing Shadows
Chasing Hearts

The Crimes of Alice
The Crimes of Alice
Hatter's Heart
Cheshire's Smile

The Mary Wiles Chronicles
Marked by Hell
Bound by Hell
Deceived by Hell
Tempted by Hell
Betrayed by Hell

Starcrossed Dragons
Riding Lightning
Grinding Frost
Swallowing Fire
Pounding Earth

Curse of the Fairy Tales
Rapunzel Untamed
Rapunzel Unveiled
Rapunzel Unchained

Her Angels
Heaven's Embrace
Heaven's A Beach
Heaven's Most Wanted

House of Durand
Indebted to the Vampires
Wanted by the Vampires
Protected by the Vampires
Embrace of the Vampires
Tempted by the Butler
Loved by the Vampires
Huntress of the Vampires
Imprisoned by the Vampires

Academy of Witches
Witching On A Star
As You Witch
Witch You Were Here
Just Witch It
Summer Witchin'

Children of the Fallen
Death In Her Eyes
Fire In Her Blood

House of Van Helsing
Her Cross To Bear
Blood Betrayed

Wicked Crown
Little Morning Star
When Hell Freezes Over
To Hell With It

The Beast of the Fae Court
Vampire CEO

Dedication

This one is for my assistant, Ashleigh, my cover artist, Krys, and my editor, Makenzie, who through all seven previous books never stopped believing in me and the Durands.

Without you three there would be no Durands. Love you!

ERIN BEDFORD

HOUSE OF DURAND
BOOK EIGHT

CHAPTER 1
Piper

A LOUD EXPLOSION CAME from the television. I jumped in my seat on the couch and the bowl of popcorn in my lap spilled over onto Darren who sat in front of me.

"Excuse me," Darren shot a pointed look back at me from where he painted my toenails a bright pink, "Am I to be your trash disposal as well as pedicurist?"

I grinned, shoving a handful of popcorn in my mouth before patting him on the head.

"Oh, don't grump. You like doing my toes. Don't pretend you don't just because the guys are here."

Darren sighed and returned to my nails while the others chuckled around us.

"It really is sad," Drake commented from his bed where he and Allister played cards. "She's got you by the dick and you don't even care."

Shifting in my seat, I tossed popcorn in Drake's direction. "That's not what you were saying the other night when I had you by the dick."

Drake smirked and licked his lips. "And I'd be more than happy to let you do it again."

"Let me, huh?" I shifted back toward the television and asked Rayne to my side, "He does know that I wear the pants in this little vampire orgy, right?"

Rayne chuckled and leaned into me, whispering in my ear, "Oh, he knows. But his manliness requires him to protest any type of dominance."

"Hey, I can hear you."

Rayne and I called out together, "We know."

"Ignore him, pet." Wynn stroked his fingers through my hair with loving strokes. "Draconius has never known the pleasure of pampering a woman. The sheer desire to see her well and truly satisfied." The way Wynn said it implied much more than a pedicure and sent tingles down to my core.

"I haven't had any complaints yet," Allister countered, his voice so full of self-confidence I had to poke fun at him.

"Yet." I turned and stuck my tongue out at him.

Drake's eyes widened and he pushed up off the twin bed and stalked toward me. "Yet, huh? Maybe I should see about that right now."

"Now, now, children," Antoine sighed from his desk on the other side of the basement. "We rarely get a night in together without some catastrophe. Can we have a single quiet evening?"

Just then the television made another loud explosion and I snort-laughed, covering my mouth to try and stifle it. Too late. As soon as I started laughing Rayne did and then the rest followed. Even Marcus who sat quietly on his bed reading a book let out a chuckle. Soon we all were laughing while Antoine simply sighed and returned to his work.

"Hehe, I needed that." I leaned my head on Wynn's shoulder, tangling my fingers in his black hair that had grown past his shoulders. I kind of liked it.

"Yeah, especially since..." Rayne trailed off.

"The vampire council is about to fry our asses?" I supplied helpfully.

"Piper," Marcus said in a warning tone.

I lifted my head off Wynn's shoulder. "What?"

"You promised no work talk tonight, remember?" Marcus's dark eyes locked with mine across the room before dropping back to his book.

"Oh, yeah. Sorry." I sank back into the couch, allowing myself one moment to bask in the presence of my men. However, my mind had other plans. It didn't take long for my mind to wander into places it shouldn't have been.

"Meet with the vampire council and tell me where they are located." Vincent, leader of the vampire hunters, had commanded me.

The fact that anyone could tell me what to do ground my gears. I had to remind myself daily that I was doing it to keep the ones I cared for safe. And Vincent promised after this one, I'd be free and the Durands would never be hunted again.

Too good to be true.

"Hey," Rayne bumped my shoulder. "That means in your head too."

I shrugged sheepishly. "I can't control what my brain does."

"Try," he rubbed my shoulders and pressed a kiss to my forehead. "There is plenty of time to worry later. Just enjoy tonight."

I nodded, trying my best to do what Rayne asked.

Rayne stiffened next to me, and I glanced over at him, his red hair falling over his eyes as he tilted his head to the side listening for something I couldn't hear even with my better than human hearing.

Leaning over to him, I touched his arm. "What is it?"

He frowned and shook his head before sighing. "Sounds like our guest is back and giving Gretchen a hard time."

I scowled and glared up at the ceiling.

Fucking Morpheus.

"Why haven't we given him over to the council?" I mused aloud, my fingers itching to get around the narcissistic vampire's throat. If it was up to me, he'd be pinned to the wall as target practice for the next century. If he couldn't keep his fangs in his mouth, then he didn't deserve to have them, especially since he was happy to let Allister take the blame.

"Piper," Antoine said my name in that tone that told me he didn't approve of what I said even if he did agree. "As enjoyable as seeing Morpheus squirm would be, we still need him. The council still believes Allister is guilty, remember."

I shot a grin at Allister. "I'm sure Allister wouldn't mind taking one for the team to put Morpheus through his paces."

Allister snorted, tossing his cards down on the bed. "As fun as that sounds, I'd like to keep my head and heart where they are. Thank you very much. However..." he sniffed and smirked. "I'm not opposed to maiming him...just a little." He pinched his thumb and pointer finger together.

"See," I jerked a hand in Allister's direction. "He gets me." I turned around on the couch, leaning over the back to plead with Antoine, jerking my foot from Darren.

"Piper," Darren scowled at me. "You're going to mess up all my hard work."

Ignoring him, I focused on Antoine. "Come on, just a little slice and dice. I promise I won't do any lasting damage..." then added with a mutter, "Not any that would matter anyway."

Antoine swiveled around in his desk chair, crossing one leg over the other. His silvery hair was loose around his shoulders the way I liked. He still wore the remnants of his suit from the day, his jacket and tie missing, and his sleeves rolled up. Just looking at him warmed my body. Especially when he looked at me like that. "As positively delightful as that sounds, I cannot in good faith allow you to do it. We need him on our side...for now."

Shoving my libido down, I pouted and crossed my arms. Spinning around on the couch, I slouched down into the cushions. "Party pooper."

"Ugh," Rayne groaned and grasped his forehead. "Someone better get up there and deal with him before Gretchen skewers him."

"I'll do it!" I jumped up, almost running Darren over in the process of getting to the stairs.

"Piper, your nails!" Darren growled, not at all bothered that I'd trampled him.

"It's fine." I waved him off. "See, they're already dry." I pointed a toe and then stuck my tongue out at him as I darted up the stairs.

Oh goodie, I get to beat up Morpheus after all. This night couldn't get any better.

CHAPTER 2
Marcus

THE BLOOD LUST IN Piper's face made me proud. Who knew someone so small could be so fierce? She was almost more deadly than any of us combined, especially since she has been training every day.

It made me happy that she has found her strength and place among us. And yet, I worried for her. I did not want her whole life to be violence and bloodshed. Piper was a beautiful woman who, as Wynn had stated, deserved to be adored and pampered. She should not be the one keeping us safe. It just wasn't right.

"Someone best go with her or she'll quite literally have Morpheus pinned to the kitchen table." Wynn mused, surveying his nails not seeming particularly worried about the club owner's safety.

There was a thud from above and all of us, even Wynn, jumped to our feet. Another bang and then a curse from Piper and we were rushing up the stairs.

"Ten to one she's already bloodied him," Drake commented from the back.

"I'll take that bet." Allister commented. "There's no way she hasn't stabbed him at least. I say she's cut off a limb."

Rayne snorted, pushing the basement door open. "Neither of you know our girl like me."

"We'd know her better if we could read her mind too," Drake pointed out, trying to shove his way forward. "Come on, move. I don't want to miss the action."

"I think you mean, you wish to stop it, correct Draconius?" Antoine called out in his commanding tone that made us all still.

Drake flinched, turning back toward our leader. "Uh, sure. Yeah. That's what I meant of course." He let out a nervous chuckle and dragged a hand through his short dark hair. "But you gotta admit...it's pretty funny."

Antoine walked between us, shifting us out of the way as he made his way to the top of the stairs. "You will not encourage her. She has not had the wrath of the vampire council down on her and we want to keep it that way."

"Are they really that bad?" Rayne questioned standing by the basement door already in the dining room.

"I had forgotten you have never come in contact with the council." Antoine pursed his lips and closed his eyes. A dish breaking broke whatever he was thinking about and turned away from Rayne. The conversation put on pause for the time being while we continued on to the kitchen.

The sight that greeted us was a surprising and yet amusing sight. Though, I would expect nothing less from Piper.

Morpheus scrambled away from Piper and Gretchen as they threw dishes at his head, each one crying out in excitement when one of them hit him. Shards of previously broken glass decorated the floor around Morpheus as he tried to fend off their attacks.

Drake moved to assist. Antoine held up his hand to hold him back. Seemed he wanted to see how it would play out as well.

"I only meant to get a taste," Morpheus explained as a dish bounced off his hand covering his face. "I wasn't going to kill her. I swear."

Piper scoffed, tossing a teacup up and down in her hand, the other on her hip as she glared down at the vampire. "Yeah, sure. And I'm sure you intended it to be the most thrilling thing she's ever done." Morpheus opened his mouth likely to lie before Piper cut him off, gripping the teacup tight in her fist. "You forget, I've been at your tender mercy before."

Morpheus had the decency to flinch at her words. "I don't kill the help. I mean, who would take out the trash if we didn't have them?" He gestured to Gretchen in a last-ditch effort.

Gretchen gaped at him, stepping forward. "I'll have you know, I am the cook. Not the trash person. You'd do well to get it right else you end up on the chopping block." A wicked gleam glinted in Gretchen's eyes that made even me feel pity for the vampire.

Finally noticing our presence, Morpheus turned to us. "Antoine, please. Call off your pet. You know I didn't mean any harm."

Antoine tucked his hands into his pockets and turned to our cook. "Are you alright, Gretchen?"

The plump older woman jerked her head in a nod. "Yes. Thanks to Piper here. Never thought I'd see the day a vampire squealed like a pig at the sight of a human woman." Her lips curled up into a positively gleeful expression.

Piper wrapped an arm around the older woman and laid her head on top of hers. "No one messes with my Gretchen." She shot a sharp look at Morpheus. "No one."

"Yes, yes. Very well. Apologies and all that. I will take my dining elsewhere tonight." Morpheus inched up to his knees, brushing the mixture of glass and porcelain off himself.

"That you will," Antoine commented in a tone that left no room for argument. If anything, it seemed as if he were angry at the vampire. The barely held back anger in his tone made the club owner wince and turned promptly toward the back door.

"Oh, and Morpheus," Piper called after him. "Be sure they are willing victims. Or I'll know."

Whether or not Morpheus believed her remained to be seen. The club owner scurried out of the house like the rat I'd always thought he was.

"Piper," Darren chastised, stepping over the piles of glass. "Not the fine China." He went to the back room and grabbed a broom and dustpan. The butler swept up the mess without having to be asked. He was good about things like that.

"Sorry, Darren." Piper hopped up on the counter, swinging her bare feet back and forth.

"Don't step back down until I'm done." Darren warned her with a pointed look. She grinned cheekily in response.

I envied them. Their easy back and forth. I wasn't so good with words. At least not when it came to Piper. The women I usually went for were easy to read. Easy to know exactly what they wanted and how to give it to them. Piper wasn't like that. What she wanted from me I had no idea. She had all these men already. What else could she possibly want or need from me?

"Hey," Rayne bumped my arm. "Don't think like that. You're worth more than you think."

Scowling at the red head, I snapped, "Don't read my mind."

Rayne shrugged and shook his hair over his eyes. "Just trying to help."

"I don't need it, nor have I asked for it."

Holding his hands up, Rayne backed out of the kitchen. "Alright, man. My bad."

"I'd say that I won this one." Drake held his hand out to his twin with a broad grin on his face. "Pay up."

Allister scowled. "No way. You don't know if Piper or Gretchen was the one who bloodied him. For all we know both of us lost."

"Oh, come on. Don't act like that. You know I won. Just pay up." Drake followed his brother out of the kitchen still arguing about who won.

"Another night wasted on nonsense." Antoine sighed and turned a sharp look on Piper. "You better make sure every single scrap of glass is picked up before you step off that counter. I don't want to have to worry about you being injured when you meet the council."

Piper grinned mischievously. "Yes, sir."

Antoine gave her a meaningful look that made her scent of arousal spike the air.

Wynn hummed and glanced around the room before commenting, "I think I will see if the others would like to play a game of cards. There must be some way to salvage this night."

"Oooh," Piper shifted on the counter to jump down, and I was there in an instant grabbing her in my arms. "Oh. Uh. Thanks."

I peered down at her. So tiny in my arms. So breakable. And yet she wasn't. Piper was so strong. Stronger than any of us it seemed. However, not in the conventional sense. How could she be so strong on the inside and yet so weak on the outside?

"Uh, Marcus," Piper chuckled nervously. "You can put me down now."

I glanced over at Darren who gave me a nod. "You should put your shoes on. Just in case."

Piper smiled shyly at me. "Are you worried about me getting hurt, Marcus?"

Brushing her hair away from her face, I murmured, "Always."

"About the glass or the council?" Piper gripped my arms a little more tightly, not in any rush to let me go even though she had told me I could.

"Can it be both?"

Lifting herself up to wrap her arms around my neck, she pressed her lips to the side of my cheek. Piper didn't immediately move away when she was done, hovering over my skin as if she wanted to do more.

"This is awkward," Piper muttered, licking her lips and pulling back.

I lowered her to the ground. One glance around the kitchen told me we were alone. I stepped back from her, giving both of us space. "You know, you don't have to do this. No one would blame you."

Piper frowned, her brows furrowed. "Do what?"

"Force yourself to be with all of us."

Cocking her head to the side, Piper gaped at me. "Is that what you think I'm doing?"

I simply stared at her. Which apparently was not the right thing to do. One moment I was looking at her and then next I was doubling over a pain in my most sensitive parts.

"What. The. Fuck. Is. Your. Problem?" Piper snarled at me, stalking out of the kitchen.

Grabbing at myself, I grunted in response. A chuckle near the kitchen door had me looking up.

Rayne leaned against the doorway with a sadistic grin. "Are you sure you don't want my help now?"

CHAPTER 3

Piper

I REWRAPPED THE BANDAGE around my hand, jerking it tighter the more I thought about the mess we were in.

The vampire council. What a load of shit. So far, they haven't done anything for our family. They weren't there for the problems we had with the master. Or when the guys were on the run from the hunters. I shouldn't expect them to be worth a shit now.

Especially, since they're the ones behind framing Allister and the financial problems.

"You're going to cut off the circulation to your hand if you keep pulling it like that," Rayne commented from the doorway of the training room.

I grunted in response and kept tugging.

Rayne walked across the room and knelt before me, grabbing my hand between his own. "Stop it, Piper. Hurting yourself isn't going to do anyone any good right now."

I huffed and let him rewrap my hands. This time looser. "I know. I'm just so frustrated right now."

"We all are." Rayne bent his head over my hands, his red hair falling over his face. "That's no excuse."

I wrinkled my nose at him.

"Don't look at me like that." Rayne lifted his head with a straight face.

I snorted. "You have a third eye now too?"

One side of Rayne's lips tugged up. "No, I just know you."

"Do you now?" I jerked on my hands, pulling him close to my face. "And what do you know?"

Rayne pressed his forehead to mine so that our breath mingled. "That you're going to worry yourself sick thinking about this. You can't do everything yourself."

"I know." I tried to pull away. Rayne cupped the sides of my face, keeping us nose to nose.

"No, you don't," Rayne insisted. "You take on everything yourself and never leave anything for the rest of us to do. Taking on the hunters by yourself. Getting yourself roped into being their lap dog. Attacking Morpheus. And now, trying to deal with the council on your own."

I growled and shoved away from him. "What else am I supposed to do? I'm trying to protect you." I jerked my arm in the air. "All of you."

"We didn't ask you to protect us." Rayne closed the distance between us. "We're supposed to protect you, not the other way around."

"And shit all that did. Going on the run. Leaving me and Darren to fend for ourselves."

"Don't tell me you're still pissy about that." Rayne scowled. "Why are you being like this? It can't just be the vampire council getting under your skin."

I shook my head and jerked on my ponytail. "It's just so much all the time. I feel like we're always running. Always fighting. Just to exist." I sighed and pressed my back to the mirrored wall before sinking down to the ground, my knees drawn up. "I'm so tired of it."

Rayne stared at me for a long moment before slowly moving across the room. "What are you saying? Do you want to leave?"

I glowered at him. "Can't you just read my mind?"

"I can but I'd rather you tell me." Rayne sank to the ground before me. Not touching me, just sitting before me.

I stared at him, trying to get my mind together and emotions in control. I didn't know why I was so angry. Why I wanted to fight so much.

"It's probably because you're used to being able to beat your problems up." Rayne shook his head and let out a hard breath. "You can't use violence to fix this."

"Why not?" I pouted, beating my fists against my knees. "Just a few minutes with them alone and this could all be over."

Rayne snorted. "As fun as that would be to see, the council isn't like anything you've ever been up against before. They have powers..."

"So," I cocked a brow. "So, do you all? That's nothing new."

Shaking his head, Rayne grabbed my hands. "No, not the same. They have powers even greater than ours. Even Antoine is hesitant to go up against them."

I frowned.

Well, that's not good. Antoine was the strongest of them all. If he was nervous about this, then we were in real trouble.

Groaning, I leaned my head on my knees. "Can we just move somewhere far far away? Like Tahiti?"

Rayne chuckled. "That sounds nice. Sadly, running isn't an option here. We have to see this through."

"We can't see anything through until we find the council. Are we sure they're going to contact us?"

Rayne lifted my hands to his lips, kissing each one in turn. "Antoine has it under control. He's sure they will contact us shortly. He's dealt with them before."

I nodded numbly.

We had heard absolutely nothing since Morpheus showed up on our doorstep and killed Jack. They killed a bunch of women and made the bartender at Club Dead point the finger at Allister. Not to mention the fact that all of the Durands' assets were in trouble.

They were playing some kind of game. A game we didn't know the rules to or know what they were trying to win. All we knew was that we couldn't lose.

The door to the training room opened and Drake poked his head in the room. "Hey we got mail."

Frowning at Drake's proclamation as he disappeared back through the door, I glanced over at Rayne before scrambling to my feet. Rayne was hot on my heels as we hurried after him.

In the foyer, Drake and the others, even Morpheus, stood together around Antoine, who was holding a fancy black envelope, the kind that unfolded from all four sides. As I approached, a pure white piece of paper with black writing on it appeared.

"What is it?" I asked, pushing around the others to get to Antoine's side.

"It's the council." Antoine held out the paper to me. It was thick like card stock and the words were handwritten in the fancy calligraphy style that I always envied.

It read:

The Vampire Council requests the presence of the House of Durand on the night of the full moon. A car will be sent.

My gaze jerked up to Antoine's. "That's it? No time. Place? Just wait and we'll get you when we get you?"

"That is the council for you," Antoine took the paper back from me and handed it to Rayne to look over. "The full moon is tomorrow. We have to be prepared."

Allister grunted. "Not much of a notice, huh?"

Drake clamped a hand down on his brother's shoulder. "Don't worry. We'll straighten this out."

"Easy for you to say," Allister shrugged his hand off. "You're not being framed for murder."

"Who cares about you? What about me?" Morpheus growled and threw his hands in the air. "I'm the one who's got the hunters and the council on them."

"Oh, shut up, you big baby," I snapped, shoving between the guys to get to Morpheus. "If I had it my way, the council would be the least of your problems."

"Piper," Antoine warned, a hand on my arm, making me pause.

"That's right, bitch," Morpheus laughed. "Heel."

That was it.

I launched myself out of Antoine's grasp and threw myself onto Morpheus, grabbing a handful of that long flowing hair he was so proud of.

"Get off me, you blood whore." Morpheus howled before I bashed his head into the floor. "Fuck, get off. Antoine! Antoine!"

"Shouldn't we stop her?" someone asked.

No one answered the question allowing me to beat Morpheus a few more times before someone grabbed a hold of me pulling me back.

"No, let me kill him," I shouted, jerking at the hold on me.

"Calm down, pet." Wynn murmured from the side of me.

"We can't kill Morpheus with the council breathing down our necks. At least," Antoine stared down at the vampire. "Not yet anyway."

Morpheus grunted and touched his head where I'd bashed it into the tile, blood dripping down his face. "I'm touched. I didn't know you cared so much."

The hands on me slackened and I twisted out of their grasp. Marcus had been the one holding me. His answering frown to my glare only riled me further.

"Chill out," Allister smooth as silk words poured into my ears, pushing my anger down and replacing it with calm.

"She's going to be pissed as soon as your powers lose their effect on her," Drake commented from somewhere in the group.

"Better than having her give us more problems," Allister replied this time coming into my line of view and stroking the side of my cheek. "We can deal with a pissed off Piper easier if the rest of us aren't dead."

* * *

"What exactly do you wear to meet a vampire council?" I mused, holding my closet door open.

"Whatever looks best on you, I suppose." Darren answered from our bed, not looking up from his book.

I shot a mischievous look over my shoulder. "I think if I wear one of you it might send the wrong message."

Darren stared at me for a long minute before his eyes widened and he blushed, dropping his gaze to the bed. "Oh. Yes. Well, the second-best thing then."

I hummed and flicked through my clothes. "Have you met the council? What are they like?"

Closing his book, he sat it in his lap and looked off to the side. "I've been with the family for a long time and in all that time I have only come across the council once."

"And?"

Darren's eyes lifted to mine. "Let me just say it wasn't a walk in the park."

"That bad huh?" I grimaced, turning from the closet and walking over to the bed. I crawled up the mattress on my hands and knees. Stopping when I reached his legs, I laid my head in his lap and murmured, "Tell me it's going to be okay?"

Darren's hand stroked through my hair, sending a calm through me that I hadn't had in a long while. I was tired. Tired of running. Tired of fighting. I just wanted to live my life and not have to deal with hunters or vampire councils.

"I'm sure it will be fine. We won't let anything happen to you."

I lifted my head from his lap. "It's not me I'm worried about. It's Allister that's up for a crime he didn't commit."

Touching my cheek, Darren peered into my eyes. "I know. We will get to the bottom of this. They are trying to take down the Durands for a reason and we won't know until we talk to them. Don't forget the location of the council is the ticket to our freedom from the hunters."

"Yeah," I muttered, laying back down in his lap. "Maybe they'll take each other out and save us all the trouble."

"One could dream," Darren whispered, stroking my back up and down. "One could dream."

CHAPTER 4

Antoine

MY FINGERS TAPPED ON the invitation from the vampire council sitting on my desk and sighed. I rubbed my forehead with my free hand, closing my eyes to block out the sight of the paper before me. Things just kept getting more complicated every day. How was I supposed to protect everyone when I didn't know what was going to happen next?

"You can't."

Not opening my eyes, I answered Rayne's voice, "Just because you can read my mind doesn't give you permission to answer it."

The sound of Rayne flopping down on one of the chairs made me lift my head. I locked my gaze on the red head and scowled. "Do you mind?"

Rayne didn't smirk like I expected him to. He laced his fingers across his stomach and stared me down. "This isn't like with the hunters, Antoine."

"You think I don't know that?" I dropped my hands down to the desk and picked up the invitation, jerking it in the air. "This is the council. They won't be easily persuaded to let us work for them."

"You mean let Piper work for them."

I ignored the snap of his tone. "It kills me as much as you that Piper is putting everything on the line for us. We should be the ones protecting her, not the other way around."

Rayne shoved up out of the chair and approached my desk, slamming his hands down on the top of it. "Then why aren't we?"

Not wavering from Rayne's glare, I tossed the invitation on the desk. "I'm trying. What do you expect me to do?"

"Don't let her go."

"What?" I stared at him with a frown. "What do you mean don't let her go?"

"Don't let her go to see the council," Rayne explained with conviction.

I shook my head. "I can't do that. They'll expect our whole household. If we don't bring Piper, then they will think we are hiding something."

"We are," Rayne shouted, pounding his fist on the desk. "Do you think the reason they are doing all this to us is because they just want attention? Don't fucking pretend this isn't because of her."

"You need to calm down." I shifted back into my seat giving us some space. "Nothing is going to get solved by letting our emotions get the best of us."

"Emotions?" Rayne scoffed, shoving away from my desk and turning his back on me. He dragged a hand over his face and chuckled, a bitter sound that didn't make this any easier. He spun around and gave me the same look he did when I turned him into a vampire. Unbridled anger and sadness. "What emotions would those be? Do you even have any left after all this time?"

I let out a long breath, my fingers tightening around each other to calm myself. "Just because I choose not to let those emotions get the better of me does not mean that I lack them. I'm just as worried for Piper as you are."

"Are you?"

Before I could answer, the office door opened and Wynn walked in. He took one look at the two of us and sighed. "It seems that I am not the only one who has concerns about this meeting with the council?"

"No," I turned my eyes back to Rayne. "You're not."

Rayne stalked over to Wynn. "Tell him. Tell him that Piper shouldn't come. That we should send her away. Somewhere no one will find her."

Wynn snorted. "What? The moon?" Rayne began to protest. Wynn cut him off. "While I agree with your sentiments Rayne. The likelihood that we could hide Piper or even keep her out of this is quite low."

"Then what do we do? Nothing?" Rayne yelled at Wynn before turning on me. "You know they will blame this all on her. They'll think that the whole hunter thing is betrayal. They won't care that it's a deal to keep us safe."

"I am aware of the council's mind set." I pushed out of my chair and rounded the desk, leaning against the opposite side to face Rayne and Wynn head on. "Unfortunately, we cannot hide Piper and we cannot leave her out of this. We must face them and plead our case. Perhaps, we will find an option we did not see before."

Rayne smirked. "Or the hunters do us a favor and take them out before they can take us out."

"It's more likely we'll get caught in the crossfires of that little interaction," Wynn mused, collapsing into the chair in front of me. "I won't let them hurt her, Antoine."

Wynn wasn't lounging in the chair with his usual nonchalance. He leaned forward his elbows on his knees and his hands clasped before him under his chin. His gaze stared hard at nothing.

I stiffened at his words. "What do you mean?"

"I will fight for her. I will not let all this fall onto her shoulders. We brought her into our world and if anyone is going to try to take her out of it, I'll gladly give my life to save hers." He lifted his gaze to meet mine. "The question is...will you?"

"I will," Rayne stepped up, pumping his fist. "I'll rip out their throats if they dare lay a finger on our girl."

"Be quiet, Rayne," Wynn snapped at the redhead. "Your love and loyalty to Piper is not the one I am questioning. It is his...our fearless leader. Would you die for her?"

I rounded my shoulders and returned his stare. "I made her my human servant."

"That's not an answer," Rayne growled.

How could they even question my loyalty to Piper? Had I not shown that I cared for her? Had I not allowed her to do as she liked? Did they really think I was so heartless that I would allow her to take the fall for us all?

"You've already let her do more than enough."

I shot a glare at the youngest of all my brothers. "Do not get in my head."

Rayne gritted his teeth, his jaw clenching. "Then answer the question."

Tucking my hands into my pockets, I stared them down. "I have risked my life for Piper many times."

"And you have reaped the benefits of those risks. This time though..." Wynn shook his head, pushing up off the chair and standing a foot from me. "This time there is no benefit except Piper. Would you die to just let her live?" Wynn cut me off with a finger shoved into my chest. "No, no more dancing with words. You fuck her happily enough but - Do. You. Love. Her?"

A fiery burn built inside of me. A low growl beginning in my chest rolled out of my mouth and I had Wynn by the throat and across the room shoved up against the bookshelves causing several of the books to fall. My fangs bared inches away from Wynn's calm face.

"That's it. Get angry. Get pissed off, my friend." Wynn grabbed my arms, not worried I'd rip his face off. "Show me what really lies in your heart."

"Do you think I hide myself for my benefit?" I hissed, shoving him against the shelf just a bit harder. "Do you think I am so heart hardened that I could not possibly love her?"

"You tell me?" Wynn responded coolly.

"I feel everything she feels. Every minute. Every breath. Her fear. Her anger. Every single piece of her being. How could I be anything but completely and totally enraptured by Piper? If it would mean she'd be safe, I would end my life in a second. I'd gladly turn back time and make her leave this house if it would mean she didn't have to bear any more pain and suffering by our hands."

Wynn cocked his head to the side. "Then why don't you just have Rayne alter her mind?"

I released him and took a step back, adjusting my clothing to smooth out the wrinkles. "I'm far too selfish to let her go now. Does that answer your question?" I turned from Wynn to glare at Rayne only to be met with the tear-stained face of the very woman we were talking about. "Piper...I..." I stepped toward her, my words lost in my throat. The emotions pouring from her were so strong they made my chest ache and my eyes water.

Piper shook her head and croaked out, "You fucking idiot." She rushed across the room and threw herself into my arms, our mouths colliding in a desperate need to devour the other. I wrapped my arms around her, pulling her as tightly to my own body as I could.

The others didn't know the extent of my fear for her life. I knew the council would go after her. That they would try their best to back us into a corner and make it so that giving up Piper would be our only choice. It wouldn't happen though. I wouldn't let it. I'd go to hell and back to keep her safe.

"That's good," Rayne commented and I dragged myself away from Piper's tempting lips. "Because you might just have to."

CHAPTER 5
Piper

THERE'S A SPECIAL PLACE in hell for those who demand you come to them on such short notice. My nerves couldn't take it. Even with only a few short hours to prepare I had sweated through three shirts before I finally had to give up on trying to stay dry.

"Maybe you should stay naked until the car comes," Drake grabbed me by the waist and dragged me up against him. "Or better yet, I know just the way to relax you." He wagged his brow and his fingers playing with the strap of my bra.

"As fun as it sounds to watch you two get it on in front of me..." Rayne began from the bed as he flicked through his phone.

"Hey, no one said you had to just watch," Drake interjected, his hands cupping my ass through my jeans to grind his erection into me.

Rayne snorted. "As thrilling as the invitation is, I don't think showing up to meet the council smelling like sex is a good idea."

The bedroom door opened, and Darren appeared. "Are you almost ready?" He took one look at me in Drake's arms and pursed his lips. "We don't have time for whatever it is you're doing in here."

I grinned at him, clinging to Drake. "We weren't doing anything."

Darren arched a brow. "Uh-huh. I'm sure that's the case." He gave one more look at the lot of us before saying, "Get dressed," and left, closing the door behind him.

When he was gone, Drake returned to stroking and grinding against me, his lips finding the side of my neck. I let him for a moment before Rayne cleared his throat. I sighed. Pushing Drake's hands away from me, I stepped out of his arms.

"Unfortunately, Darren's right." I turned to the closet and grabbed the first thing I saw, a silk red sleeveless top. I moved to put it on, and Drake grabbed my hands. "What are you doing?"

"What if Darren's not right?" Drake stared down at me, the blouse between us. "Why don't we just forget the council and stay right here?"

"You can't be serious," I gaped at him, my brow furrowed. "We can't just not show up." I turned away from his grasp and pulled my shirt over my head.

"Why not?" Drake followed after me. "Why can't we just run away? Run away from all of this?"

Before I could answer, Rayne did.

"Because they would find us," he climbed off the bed and walked toward us. "If not the council, then the hunters. We can't just ignore our problems and hope they all go away. It doesn't work like that."

"And you would know, huh?" Drake snapped, he moved in close, so his height towered over Rayne. "You haven't met the council, I have. They did this for a reason and won't stop until they get what they want. Even if it means all of us are dead."

I understood Drake's concern. All of their concerns. They were afraid for me. And I was terrified for them. If I could tuck them all away to keep them safe from the hunters and the council I would. However, we tried that before and the hunters eventually found us. We couldn't keep running. We couldn't hide from our enemies. We had to stay and fight. Or at least, plead our case.

"Piper." Rayne glanced my way, not giving in to Drake's threat. "You've done enough already. It's our turn to protect you."

I huffed a laugh. "You're probably all wishing you'd left me to the master while you had the chance." I wrapped my arms around my middle and muttered, "Probably would have been a lot easier."

"No way," Drake stopped his huffing and puffing to take me by the hand. "We'd never change any of it. Not if it meant we didn't get to be with you." He lifted my hand to his mouth kissing the back of my hand. "No one liked that old coot anyway."

"Yeah," Rayne concurred. "The gnarly bastard was always on the death list. Even before you came into the picture. You just made it easier to kill him."

I cocked my head to the side and smiled. "You guys are so sweet."

"Alright, alright." Rayne lifted his hands and stepped back. "Enough with the kissy faces. Darren is out there debating how to light a fire under our asses."

As one we moved toward the bedroom door. I reached for the doorknob, and it opened before any of us could. Darren looked up as the door opened. When he saw us, he paused.

"Oh, good. You're coming. At last."

"Did you ever doubt us?" I grinned and kissed him on the forehead before skipping past.

Rayne and Drake chuckled coming in close behind me. We all filtered down the hallway and toward the stairs. At the top of the stairs, Wynn waited, looking as tantalizing as ever.

"There she is," Wynn reached for me as we approached. "I was beginning to wonder if I would have to persuade you to come down, my love."

I cozied up to him, throwing my arms around his neck. "I could still use some persuading. If you're offering."

Wynn's hand slid along my sides while our noses brushed against one another. "Oh, pet," he whispered into my mouth. "I'm always offering."

"Hey, come on now," Rayne bumped against us on his way down the stairs. "If we don't have time to screw around you two surely don't."

"I don't know what you mean, brother." Wynn released me but kept an arm around my waist, leading me down the stairs.

"What he means," Drake said, coming up behind us. "Is that you take far too long to get the job done."

I snorted, glancing over my shoulders. "And how is that a bad thing?"

Wynn tightened his grip on my waist. "I believe the lady has answered for me. However, you must praise a woman's body the way you would a goddess. For to treat her as anything less would make you less than worthy of her touch."

Drake smirked at me. "And sometimes a lady just needs a good hard fuck."

Everyone laughed until we hit the foyer where Antoine and Morpheus waited for us.

"Good to see you're all in high spirits seeing as my life is on the line," Morpheus snarled, flashing his fangs at us for having the audacity to dare to laugh in the face of danger.

I stepped away from Wynn and stopped before Morpheus, staring the club owner down. "You Morpheus are lucky to even be breathing..." I paused and smirked. "So, to speak. You are only alive by the grace of Antoine's will and that is all. If I had my way, you'd be strung up by your little parts." I flicked my hand at his crouch with a grimace. "And your guys on the ground while I danced and *laughed* on top of them."

To my delight, Morpheus's blanched, his eyes skittering over to Antoine and back to me as if the head of the house would save him in some way.

"That's enough, Piper." Antoine gave me a chastising look even as his lips twitched.

"Sir," Darren interrupted anything I might have said, standing by the intercom. "The car has arrived."

Morpheus didn't have to be told twice. He took the opportunity to put some distance between us and walked out the door, leaving me alone with my guys. Well, most of them.

I frowned and searched the foyer as if they might be hiding somewhere. "Where's Allister and Marcus?"

"Here," Allister said, coming out of the dining room. Looking him over, I noticed a tiny bit of red on the edge of his lips. Moving over to him, I reached up and brushed my thumb against the side of his lips, pulling the liquid away.

"Is that...blood?" I quirked a brow. "Couldn't wait to eat later?"

Allister shrugged a shoulder sheepishly. "Never know when it might be your last meal."

I pressed my hand flat against his face, my gaze softening. "This won't be your last meal, Allister. Not if I have anything to say about it."

He placed his hand on top of mine and squeezed it slightly. "I know. Best to hope for the best and prepare for the worst."

I nodded, dropping my hand but not letting go of his. "Come on. Let's go."

Turning around, I found myself facing the others with a determination in my blood. I would not allow my family - the one I had built and kept through blood and sweat - to fall because of some old as dirt council. They think they could frame Allister and take our money and we'd just roll over and do what they wanted? Then they hadn't been paying attention.

"What about Marcus?"

"Waiting outside," Antoine ushered me toward the door. "We can't keep the council waiting."

"Oh, we can," I responded with a sniff. "I'm just not sure how much good it will do."

CHAPTER 6
Rayne

THE THOUGHTS AROUND ME were jumbled. Everyone was worried about what was to come. Darren had stayed behind with Gretchen, though with much protest. However, someone had to be at the house in case something went wrong. Not that we had a backup plan exactly. Or at least, I didn't have one.

My gaze shifted to Antoine, trying not to draw attention to myself. His mind wasn't quite as jumbled full of thoughts as the others. The calm in his mind was almost suspicious.

Antoine's gaze lifted. His pale eyes locked with mine.

Rayne.

I gave a subtle nod. The others were too caught up in their own thoughts to notice the exchange.

If this goes wrong, you must get her away.

I stared at Antoine. How exactly did he expect me to do that?

There's a bag packed and papers in my safe. You know the code.

I shifted in my seat, scratching the back of my neck as I bobbed my head.

She'll try to sacrifice everything for us. You know she will. We can't let her this time. This time, we get her out and gone.

I wanted to ask him exactly where I was supposed to take Piper that would keep her out of the council's and the hunters' views. Except I couldn't, not now. Thankfully, Antoine filled that blank in as well.

There's instructions in the safe. If I die. So will she. You must save her. Like I saved you.

I blinked at Antoine. Not quite believing what he was saying. He wanted me to what now? Save Piper? The way he saved me? I didn't know if I could do that. It took a lot of power to change someone into a vampire. Something I never had a lot of.

You can do it. My eyes darted up to Antoine's again. He stared me down, almost daring me to deny it. *I believe in you.*

I huffed a laugh.

"What?" Piper bumped me with her arm and her brow raised. "What's so funny?"

I pressed my lips into a reassuring smile, grabbing her hand in mine. "Nothing. Just thinking about Morpheus's face when you threatened him."

The vampire in question snarled but kept his mouth shut.

Piper smirked, leaning into my side.

That's right. Yuck it up, bitch. You won't think you're so hot once the council gets a hold of you. Then we'll see who is begging for mercy.

"Hey," I kicked out, hitting Morpheus's shin with my foot. "That's my girlfriend you're talking shit about."

Piper tightened her grip on my hand. *Fucking twat waffle.*

Morpheus scowled at the two of us but didn't say anything.

Coward.

I turned my head and kissed Piper on the head. "Calm now. We don't need to arrive covered in each other's blood. That's just what they want from us."

"When will we get there?" Drake grunted, leaning forward onto his knees with his elbows. "Are they just expecting us to go in blind?"

Antoine stared out the window, his gaze scanning the area. "They don't want us to know where they're located. Except they made a mistake." Antoine shot a look in my direction. "We're not going out of town..."

Everyone shifted to see out the window better. Antoine was right. The area around us was familiar. Too familiar.

"Is that...Club Dead?"

"What?" Morpheus pushed us all out of the way to stare out the window. "It's not enough that those bastards were killing off my patrons but now they've taken over my place? Have I not suffered enough?"

"Not nearly enough in my opinion," Piper muttered, earning her a look so fierce from Morpheus that I thought for a moment he might attack her. His mind was on other things. Like the council who was responsible for all of this.

"What's the plan?" Allister asked, moving our focus from the windows to inside the car. "I mean...we have a plan, right?" When no one answered, Allister cursed and threw himself back in his seat. "So, we're doomed."

Marcus spoke for the first time since we'd left the house. "Only the one without faith is ever doomed."

Drake snorted. "Nice time to be poetic. Maybe save some of that for the council. Maybe we can talk our way out of this."

The car stopped and it was silent except for the beating of Piper's heart. It rampaged in her chest giving off how much more nervous she was than she appeared to be.

I grasped her hand in my own and squeezed it, giving her a reassuring smile.

Tell me it will be okay. Lie to me if you have to.

I leaned over and pressed my lips to her forehead murmuring, "It will be okay."

The door to the car opened before any of us could reach for it. The vampire on the other side wasn't one I recognized. His large form put even Marcus's body to shame. Though, I had to admit that I thought Marcus had more personality than this guy.

No one moved at first.

"Out," the muscle man commanded. His voice a low growl, almost like he'd smoked one too many packs of cigarettes before he became a vampire.

Not waiting to be told twice, we piled out of the car one right after the other as if we were on a death march. It felt like that was what we were doing. Marching straight to our deaths. Or that of Piper's.

We approached the front of the club where at this time of night the big red light up sign usually glared back at us. Tonight, it was eerily dark. Another muscled vampire stood at the door, blocking the entrance to the club.

I'm being led into my own club. How have I fallen so far?

I sniffed in amusement at Morpheus's thought. In any other case, it would be hilarious to see the arrogant prick brought down a few notches. However, in this case, I'd have taken dealing with Morpheus over the council.

Piper stayed at my side, the others forming a circle around her as if to guard her from the oncoming conflict. If Piper noticed, she didn't say anything, and her mind was too jumbled right then with emotions for me to pick out a certain thought. I preferred to focus on the enemies' minds in any case.

Keep your ears open.

This thought came from Antoine, and I gave a subtle nod. They were all relying on me to be able to figure out the council's play before they spring it on us. Since I'd never met the council, I wasn't sure how that would go or if I could even get into their minds.

The inside of the club hadn't changed much. Someone had moved all the couches and chairs to the sides of the room except for one. On that singular couch sat three figures. If they weren't all sitting together, I wouldn't have thought they would even know each other. They were that different.

On the right end of the couch sat a man in a purple suit lined with gold. He sat with one leg crossed over the other, a golden cane propping up his hands. The only thing missing from his ostentatious outfit was a top hat covering his dark bald head. My eyes dipped to the table in front of them.

Ah. There it is.

The top hat sat on the short table before them where three glasses of blood sat. Curiously, a baby doll was propped up against the hat with its own little glass of blood before it. Frowning, I shifted my gaze to find the vampire that might match the baby doll.

In between the two adult vampires sat a girl. Not more than nine or ten. She wore one of those lace and ruffled dresses with bows all over it. The curls of her yellow hair were pinned up on each side and a pale blue ribbon adorned her hair. Her big blue eyes, pert nose, and pouty mouth made her look innocent, harmless.

One look in those eyes said otherwise. Old and soulless were the only emotions, there was not a shred of mercy in that doll-like face.

Or a thought. I frowned. I couldn't read any of them. Not the purple suit guy. Not the undead child. Not even the...I pursed my lips at the last figure. This one was completely normal looking. Almost too normal. The man could be anybody. The guy at the grocery store. The soccer dad. You couldn't pick this guy out of a line up. He was so ordinary.

He was wearing khakis for god's sake!

What a group of freaks!

It took everything in me not to laugh at Piper's assessment of the three people before us.

The two muscle heads led us until we stood before the three of them, the table between us. That creepy doll staring up at us as if it too was judging us.

"Welcome House of Durand," the man in purple spoke, leaning forward on his cane as his pitch-black eyes scanned us with increasing interest. "Thank you for taking the time out of your busy lives to visit with us."

"Like we had a choice," Piper muttered to herself, causing Drake and myself to cough as we tried to cover our laugh. Antoine lifted his gaze to the ceiling as if praying for patience. Either from him or the council before us.

"Oh, fucking hell. She's going to get us all killed," Morpheus cried, pushing between us to stand at the front. "Look," he bent at the waist, bowing to the council, his hands pressed together before him. "I'm innocent in all this. I'm a simple club owner. I pay my dues. I don't draw attention to myself." He waved behind him at us. "It's them you want. They're the traitors. It's them you want."

The three council members stared at him with distaste.

Piper snorted. "You should have let me kill him when we had the chance."

A giggle like a chime of bells filled the room. The little girl jumped off the couch and skipped around the table. Everyone froze as she approached Piper, grabbing her by the hand and smiling, her little fangs glinting in the light.

"Uh, hi," Piper looked down at the girl.

The girl giggled again. "I like you. You're funny."

Piper glanced at me and the others, a silent cry for help before turning back to the girl. "Uh...thanks?" Piper locked eyes with me shoving her thoughts at me so hard I winced. *What the fuck?*

I peered down at the little girl squinting my eyes as I tried to read her thoughts. But there was nothing. An emptiness that couldn't possibly be.

The little girl turned her big orbs on to me with a pout. "You shouldn't peek at a girl's thoughts. It's not polite."

I didn't bother denying what I'd done, simply shrugged.

"Your little parlor trick will not work on us." The man in purple smirked, gesturing his cane toward the other man. "Caleb here has tricks of his own. Including protecting us against other vampire abilities. I wouldn't try any of your puny little powers against us. You will surely fail."

Well, we're fucked.

CHAPTER 7
Piper

THE ROOM COULDN'T BE more quiet than after mister purple people eater made his groundbreaking announcement. He basically said we are powerless before them. All because of this guy Caleb who could have been my creepy uncle.

Then there was the undead child bride latched onto my hand. What the hell was up with that? Like, weren't there rules against making children into vampires? If not, there should be. It was just beyond fucking freaky.

"My apologies," the purple people eater stood and gave a theatrical bow. "We have not been properly introduced. I am Tuma. And you have already been introduced to Caleb and the little darling before you is..."

"Odette," the undead child bride announced quite happily. "And you're Piper."

I forced a smile. "Yes, I'm Piper."

"Come on, you can sit by me." She tugged me by the hand, stronger than I'd have expected from a child of her age but not of a vampire. I had no choice but to follow, glancing over my shoulder at the guys for some kind of tip or help of some kind.

Odette led me to the other side of the table and the other two made room for me to sit between Odette and purple people eater, excuse me Tuma. Though, I couldn't complain. I'd rather have the monster who looks like what he is than the one who conceals himself behind normality.

Purple people eater shifted his body toward me, throwing an arm around the back of the couch. "Now that we are all cozy just like family. Why don't we discuss why we are here?"

"This is my dolly..." Odette picked up her doll completely ignoring Tuma's words. "Her name's Fiona." She beamed up at me waiting for me to answer.

I forced a smile. "She's very nice."

Odette flashed her fangs at me. "My mommy gave her to me. As a gift. I love my mommy." She said it in such a creepy way while she stroked her doll's blonde hair. It was almost a replica of the girl herself.

I flicked my eyes toward the guys who were a mixture of apprehension and fear. Only Antoine seemed perfectly at ease. Which was funny since I was confused as all get out. What the hell was going on here?

Turning my attention back to Odette, I asked, "And where is your mommy?"

Odette smiled calmly at her doll before peering up at me. "I ate her."

Well...uh...okay.

I thought perhaps I'd have an ally in the undead child bride, but it seems like she might just be the psycho of the bunch. The only one who seemed remotely like they might see some reason was the purple people eater.

Shifting, I asked Tuma, "You were saying? About why we were here?"

"It seems that we have a little bit of a problem here." Tuma tapped his cane on the heel of his shoe. "While I have no issue with you, Miss Piper. You have taken care of some of our more sensitive problems before we even knew they were problems."

"Okay..." I drew in a breath, leveling my eyes on the guys before turning back to Tuma. "So, what's the problem?"

"Are you having sex with all these men?"

I stiffened at the sound of Caleb's voice. A neutral tone with no emotional inflection whatsoever. Shifting in place, I confronted the vampire. "Excuse me?"

Caleb turned his brown eyes onto me, his facial expression not changing in any way. "If I am correct in my information and I always am, you are having sexual intercourse with all of the Durand vampires."

A throat cleared, I thought it was Drake, but it was Marcus who answered, "Not all of us."

I shot a look at Marcus, who didn't so much as acknowledge me. I was two seconds away from kicking him in the nuts again. At this rate, he'd be lucky to use his parts let alone get them anywhere near me.

"Very well," Caleb conceded. "Five of the six vampires of the House of Durand have a sexual relationship with you."

I frowned, not understanding where this line of questioning was going. "And your point is?"

"Have you been coerced or are you just a whore?" Caleb's eyes zeroed in on me as if he wanted to destroy my very soul. It was the first emotion I had gotten from him - if you could call it emotion.

There was a movement on the other side of the room. Drake and Rayne both tried to move forward but were stopped by the others. Marcus and Allister held onto the shoulders of Drake while Antoine held onto Rayne with a simple hand on his arm. The warning in Antoine's eyes told them to keep their cool. I was with him. They were playing with us. Trying to get a reaction out of us.

They wanted to play? Fine. Let's play.

I crossed one leg over the other and peered over at Caleb with my best seductive pout. "What? A girl can't have a little fun with her immortality?"

"You are hardly immortal," Caleb countered with a tight jaw. His gaze slid over to Antoine. "You are nothing more than what your master has made you. Take him away, and what do you have left?"

The hair on my arms stood on end as Caleb focused all his attention on Antoine. Something was happening. Something not good.

Antoine didn't react for a moment. His face as unbothered as ever by the threat ahead of him. Then he was writhing on the floor, grabbing his head. I jerked to get up and then let out a gasp of pain as Odette tightened her grip on my hand to where I thought she might actually break it.

"Stop it," I snapped, my voice breaking as I said it. "Please, stop it."

"If Antoine dies, then you die and all our problems are solved," Caleb stated his focus never wavering off of Antoine.

"Now, now, Caleb." Tuma tut-tutted. "We cannot destroy them simply for a personal dislike for the accused." Caleb didn't listen to Tuma for a moment and then the purple people eater said his name once more, just once, in a way that even I would not dare to disobey.

Finally, after what seemed like a lifetime of watching Antoine cry out in pain, his eyes blindly searching around him for something to stop the agony, Caleb blinked, dropping his gaze from Antoine. Marcus went to Antoine's side where I wanted to be but didn't dare try to get to him. Odette still had a tight grip on my hand, her tiny little nails drawing blood from where they clawed at me.

Odette lifted my hand, her eyes finding mine as her small tongue darted out and licked the blood that dripped out. "Oh," her eyes widened in surprise. "I do see why they like you so much. You taste good."

I grimaced. "Uh, thanks. Can I have my hand back now?"

Odette looked like she wanted to say no.

Tuma cut in before she could answer. "Odette give Miss Piper her hand back."

Pushing her lower lip out in a pout, Odette released me, her gaze settling on the vampires before her. She slipped off the couch and walked around the table to stand before the six of them. She swayed back and forth with her hands behind her back, so her skirt moved like a little bell.

"They're very pretty," Odette glanced over her shoulder at me. "Do you love them?"

Hesitant to tell them any of my weaknesses, I kept silent. Only when Tuma said, "I too wish to know how this relationship works," I dared to answer.

I cleared my throat and met Odette's gaze. "I love them."

"How?" Odette asked curious as the child she portrayed yet the years in her eyes told a different story. "How can you stretch your love to cover them all? Is it not painful?"

My brow furrowed at her question. "Love is not something that is limited. If it's painful, then it isn't love."

"Are you sure?" This question came from Caleb, who looked sharply at the Durands and then me. "Hasn't the house of Durand caused you nothing but pain and suffering since the day you met them? You even cut yourself the very first day of your employment."

I gaped at Caleb, closing the hand that held the scar from the broken vase. "How...how do you know that?"

Tuma brushed my hair away from my face, drawing my attention to him. "Caleb is quite well versed in the ways of the mind. He can not only read what is in the minds of others but manipulate it so that they only know what he wished them to know."

"It is easy to slip in a suggestion or two into the minds of others," Caleb explained, his eyes locked on mine. "Even so much as to suggest one saw something they did not." His lips ticked at that phrase giving away his guilt at turning the bartender against us.

"Or even making a company sell their shares to the lowest bidder." Odette giggled and danced around the Durands as if she were hearing some music the rest of us did not.

"Why?" I questioned my head pivoting around from one of the council members to the other. "Why are you doing this to us?"

"Can you not think of anything?" Tuma quirked a brow, a hint of his fangs showing as he smiled at me. "While we commend you on taking out Boris and his blood trading, we cannot overlook your assistance to the hunters."

"Hey," I jumped up shaking a finger at him. "There's a reason for that. We were on the run. We didn't have a choice."

"There is always a choice," Caleb responded with a calm that frightened me.

I gritted my teeth.

They weren't going to listen to me. They'd already made up their mind. Now they just wanted to watch us squirm and beg. I would not give them the satisfaction of either.

"Nothing else to say?" Tuma asked, tapping his cane against his shoe.

I crossed my arms over my chest and glowered. "Why? You will do what you want regardless of what I have to say. So why bother?"

"While you may have succumbed to your fate, your masters have not." Caleb's attention followed me as I walked back to my men.

Odette paused at my side before skipping back over to the other two council members. "I like her and them." She flopped down on the couch and kicked her feet back and forth. "I think we should keep them."

"They are not dolls for your collection Odette." Caleb chastised the child.

She snarled at Caleb in turn her innocent features turned fierce. "Unlike you I do not wish to turn every being's mind into mush."

"Odette is correct." Tuma interrupted their squabbling. "They are too valuable to just kill outright and yet they cannot be unpunished for the crimes they have committed against their own kind."

"And him?" Caleb pointed at Morpheus who had stayed off to the side no doubt hoping to hide in the background.

Tuma looked at Morpheus, his lips ticked with displeasure. It must have been some kind of sign because Odette grinned so broadly her fangs were exposed. "Kill him."

CHAPTER 8

Piper

THE LOOK ON MORPHEUS'S face was priceless. If I could bottle up this moment and keep it forever, I would have in an instant., Unfortunately, I only had this moment and I was going to enjoy it while I could.

"Kill me?" Morpheus choked out, grabbing at his face and neck. "Please…your excellencies, I have been nothing but a faithful servant to the council for many many years." He lowered himself down to his knees, his voice becoming cracked and pained. "You would kill me while you would let these t…traitors go?"

Tuma jerked to his feet. "You would dare question the council's decisions?"

Morpheus held his hands up, his eyes wide. "No, no. Of course not. I am simply wishing to know what grievance I have committed to cause my sentence to be so…permanent?"

Tuma walked toward Morpheus, his cane clacking on the floor with each step. "Not only have you betrayed your own kind by passing information about one to the other, but you have on more than one occasion been reported to have been conducting illegal blood activities here at your club."

The club owner's mouth dropped open.

Illegal blood activities? I couldn't fathom what that could be. Knowing Morpheus, it was probably worse than anything I could imagine.

"Furthermore," Tuma continued.

SPLAT.

I blinked at the thick chunks that were once Morpheus's brain as it slid down my face. I swiped a hand over my face trying to clear as much of it off all the while thinking, "Don't freak out, don't freak out."

The others were hardly bothered by the sudden explosion of Morpheus's head, each of them shifting away with distaste while Odette giggled and clapped her hands. Tuma sighed begrudgingly and turned to Caleb.

"You could have at least let me finish."

Caleb angled his head to the side. "Why? You need not explain yourself to him. And besides the vote was two to one as it were. He was going to die either way. I simply sped things along."

"Still there is an order to these things you cannot simply..."

While Tuma and the other council members argued over how long to wait to kill someone when they have been sentenced, I couldn't keep my eyes off the headless body of Morpheus.

Blood and gore shouldn't bother me. It wasn't exactly anything new. I'd cause quite a bit of it myself. Except for some reason having someone I knew - even if it was someone I hated - killed just like that without moving a muscle made my stomach roll.

Tuma said my name but it was as if it were muffled. I could barely hear it over the thundering of my own heart. The room felt hot and I feared I'd sweat through my clothes once again. How embarrassing.

"Miss Piper," Tuma's voice came through more this time. I blinked up at the vampire who seemed quite concerned.

I blinked a bit more, turning my head from side to side to see everyone staring at me. The guys had moved in close to me but not touching me while Odette stared curiously at me. Caleb didn't seem to give two shits about me. Not that I expected him to.

"I'm alright, thank you." The guys weren't so convinced. I waved them off as Tuma moved back to his seat.

"My apologies for the mess," Tuma grimaced at the remains of Morpheus as if it hadn't just been one of them. "Where were we?"

I licked my lips, my mouth felt like I'd swallowed Cotton balls. "Discussing our punishment?"

"Ah, yes," Tuma breathed, crossing his legs once more. "What do we do about you seven?"

"I like them," Odette piped in with a gleam in her eyes. "I want to keep them."

"Now, now, Odette," Tuma clicked his tongue. "They are people not dolls."

"I am curious to how this arrangement works." Caleb circled his fingers before him, staring at all of us in a kind of deranged manner. As if we were some kind of circus freaks.

"I do not understand what you don't understand about it." Antoine finally graced us with something helpful to say. "She belongs to us and we to her."

"And you love her?" Caleb asked, his head tilting even further to the side. "How curious."

Odette snorted. "Just because you have the emotional capacity of my dolly doesn't mean that others do." She clutched her doll to her chest. "Besides, I think it's romantic."

"Yes..." Tuma trailed off, he bobbed his foot up and down. "I do wonder how the seven of you were able to fall for one another.

Was it some twist of fate or are you simply victims of your circumstances?"

"No offense meant, your excellencies," Wynn stepped in, placing a hand on my waist. "I would not call us victims of any kind. We have fallen for Piper because of who she is not because we were looking for someone to share or that we are only victims of happenstance. I would love Piper Billings even if we had not been in any kind of mortal danger."

"And the rest of you?" Tuma pointed his cane at the others. "Do you feel the same way?"

A collective movement had the others closing in around me, each of them placing a hand on me in some way. I tried to keep my mind clear so as not to give this Caleb guy any reason to doubt our words. They didn't know about Darren it seemed in their infinite knowledge. Or about Marcus and I not quite being there yet.

Crap don't think about it. Shit balls. Fuck.

Caleb made a sound in his throat that could have possibly been a laugh. My eyes jerked up to study him. Suspicion set in as he spoke.

"Would you bet your lives on it?"

"Excuse me?" Antoine asked, the tone of his voice to others would have seemed like he could be there all day. Only those closest to him would know the tick at his lip that gave away how short his patience was getting.

"Yes, that is a brilliant idea." Tuma laughed, clapping his hands twice. "It would answer our curiosity and give us time to think of an appropriate punishment for your transgressions."

Frowning, I glanced from one of the council members to the others. "I don't understand."

"It's like a game!" Odette beamed, clasping her hands together. "Like Cinderella finding her prince times six!"

"Yes," Tuma drew out. "I do believe I like this idea. Caleb...if you would."

Caleb stood from the couch and approached us. I backed away from him not wanting to end up like Morpheus on the ground there.

"Miss Piper, please relax. He's not going to hurt you." Tuma laughed but I wasn't convinced.

"Yeah right. Tell me what's going on?" I finally was getting tired of these games and wanted to know what they were going on about.

"You claim that you would have fallen for each other regardless of all the events that have happened. We want you to prove it," Tuma explained with a nod.

I inched back from Caleb's outstretched hand. "And how exactly am I supposed to do that?"

"I'm going to erase your memories," Caleb said plainly.

"Uh...no? I don't think so. I like my memories right where they are. Thanks all the same." I shook my head back and forth, falling into the guys as Caleb pursued me.

"Do not worry, Piper," Odette giggled. "They won't be gone. Just..." she paused searching for the word.

"Suppressed," Caleb answered for her. "I will suppress all memory of your relationship with the Durands. It will be as if you were just beginning your service to them."

I blinked at him. "But why?"

Tuma tut-tutted. "We want you to show us. That you would still fall in love with each other if you weren't in mortal danger."

I blinked once more. "But why?"

Tuma's lips curled up into an amused grin. "Call it morbid curiosity." When I didn't answer, he sighed. "Indulge us this once, it may be in your favor."

"Piper." Antoine took my hand and drew me forward. "I do believe we should do this for the council."

I pressed my lips together wanting to argue but not sure how to go about it in front of the council. Antoine inclined his head slightly, his eyes telling more than just the nod. Do this and we might get out of this. Do this and we just might not end up like Morpheus.

My eyes flickered to the ground where the body still laid and then back up to Tuma. "How long do we have?"

"A week," Caleb answered quickly.

I scoffed, sneering at him. "Could you fall in love with one person let alone six in one week?"

"Very well," Tuma answered, and then hummed as he tapped his chin with his ring-covered fingers. "A month. One month for each of them. That gives you half a year to prove to us that you can fall in love with each of them without choosing just one."

How could I get out of this? Could I get out of this? Was it even possible to fall in love with them all over again in that short of time? I mean, I kind of did it before, right? How hard could it be?

I swallowed thickly, glancing at the others for a moment before locking eyes with Caleb. "Fine. I'll do it."

CHAPTER 9

Antoine

IN MY EXPERIENCE, IN the presence of the council it was best to listen and wait for the right moment to come before taking advantage of the situation. If the council liked you then they would make you jump hoops just to save face but no real punishment would be doled out.

My eyes dropped to Morpheus's prone form. Or what was left of him. Morpheus had gone about the whole thing wrong. Pleading and begging had never swayed the council. Accusations and finger pointing would get you an even swiffer death. Playing along with their little games as Piper had done was the only way to leave this place alive.

While the council may not be as old as my master Boris, they grew bored of immortality like the rest of us and have to find their entertainment in some way.

Enter us.

I had anticipated something like this would happen. Not this exact scenario. I never expected them to be so curious about our relationship. It wasn't abnormal for the humans serving the vampires to be shared between the family. Perhaps not in the capacity Piper did. They certainly didn't love their blood whores. And Piper would have my balls if I ever referred to her as such.

"I'll do it."

My head jerked to my human servant, Piper, the love of my life. I know I had encouraged her to do as they wanted but I never expected her to do it so easily. I at least thought she would put up more of a fight. Whine a little bit or something. Perhaps she too saw the direness of our situation.

Caleb reached out his hand to touch her. I grasped his wrist before he could so much as place a finger on her.

"Hold on, if you please," I immediately replied to Caleb's questioning look.

"Do you have an objection?" Caleb's bored tone would have me believe that he could care less about the whole thing. The tension in his arm where I held him said differently.

"If this is a test to see if Piper will fall for all of us again, then it would be disproportionate in the fact that she is my human servant. She will be automatically drawn to me more than the others."

"Ah," Tuma mused from his place on the couch. "I could see how that would be unfair. It would probably behoove you to repress her bond to Antoine as well as her enhanced senses." He grinned so that one fang flashed as he chuckled. "It would be quite a surprise to wake up tomorrow with superhuman powers, wouldn't it Miss Piper?"

Piper smiled weakly. "It would be preferable not to have a panic attack because I accidentally broke something."

"Wouldn't be her first time," Drake muttered, earning him a glare from Piper.

Odette giggled at our exchange, kicking her feet happily. "I can't wait to see how it all turns out." She cocked her head to the side and grinned maliciously. "If you fail, maybe Tuma will let me keep you after all."

Knee quaking fear shot into me from Piper. She really did not like Odette. Not that I blamed her. Making child vampires was forbidden. Particularly because of the one before us. They did not develop the way they should and so their needs do not gear toward the normal. One does not want to be at the mercy of one of the children of the undying.

I cleared my throat, turning everyone's attention back to the task at hand. "Well, then, shall we proceed?"

Piper's relief poured into me. Curious how she would prefer her mind meddled with than play with Odette.

"May I?" Caleb cleared his throat and I realized I was still holding his wrist.

I released him and inclined my head, stepping back from him.

Caleb placed a hand on the side of Piper's forehead and murmured, "Just relax. This shouldn't hurt."

"Shouldn't?" Piper squeaked, her suspicion flittered into me and I had to agree.

I kept my eyes on Piper as I watched Caleb work, focused on Piper's emotions the entire time. Her fear stayed steady for a few moments then slowly as if falling asleep her emotions calmed and then there was nothing. I didn't feel her at all.

Rayne was there first to catch her before Piper collapsed onto the floor.

"Why did she pass out?" Rayne demanded, holding her close and checking her breathing. "What did you do to her?"

"Nothing that I didn't say I was going to do." Caleb stated matter-of-factly, dropping his hand to his side. "Her mind needs time to reorganize. It's best done while unconscious."

"And the bond between us?" I asked, apprehension filling me with more dread than I was willing to admit. For the first time in I couldn't even remember how long now - it was as if Piper had always been there in the back of my heart beating a tune just for me - now the place she sat was empty leaving Darren's constant worry behind.

"It is merely suppressed just as her memories," Caleb continued to explain. "Deleting memories is easy, restoring them is near impossible. It is much more convenient to lock them away."

"What happens if they come back?" Marcus thankfully asked.

"That won't happen."

"But what if it does?" Rayne reiterated, not taking Caleb's answer. "Will that make the whole test null and void? How will we be punished if your abilities are not up to par?"

Caleb stalked over to Rayne coming face to face with the red head. Annoyance pinched his eyes as he flashed his fangs at Rayne. "That. Won't. Happen."

"Now, now, Caleb." Tuma waved the other man off. "It is a sensible question."

Visibly forcing himself to calm, Caleb stepped back from Rayne and folded his arms over his chest. "The likelihood of her memories resurfacing is slim to none. However," Caleb interrupted before Rayne could ask again, "If by chance, they do reappear you may contact me to have them repressed until the test has concluded."

"And how do we contact you?" Wynn questioned, coming to Piper's side. "How will you know the test has been completed?"

Caleb smirked. "I'll know."

Before anyone could press further, Tuma stood from the couch. He leaned over and picked up his glass from the table, touching his drink for the first time since we'd been there. "Sunrise will come soon. You will want to clean Miss Piper up and put her to bed before you make your preparations for the coming months. We thank you for giving us your time."

Tuma lifted his glass to us before drinking from it, turning his back on us. Odette chatted to her doll completely ignoring us while Caleb took one last look at Piper, an arrogant look on his face that I couldn't figure out and then walked out of the room.

We had been dismissed as easily as we had been called. I nodded to the others who with reluctance headed for the door. Rayne lifted Piper into his arms with Marcus and Wynn close to her sides. The twins led the way with me bringing up the rear.

"Antoine," Tuma's voice called out before I could leave with the others.

I paused. "Yes, your excellency?"

Tuma picked up his hat and sat it on his head, adjusting the brim just so. "I have always admired you. You broke away from your master which is no simple feat. You've made yourself a small empire and even the hunters fear you. I would hate for you to lose all that over a simple woman."

My lips curled up, making Tuma's brows raise in question. "Piper has been called many things. Simple is not one of them. She'd be insulted to hear as much."

Tuma chuckled. "I did get that impression."

"As far as ruining everything, what is the point of living forever if you must do it alone?"

Tuma tipped his hat to me and I took that as my turn to be dismissed. I headed back outside to where the others were waiting by the car. Piper had been placed inside already with Rayne and Wynn. Marcus and the twins waited outside for me.

"What did the doctor want?" Drake asked, his arms crossed over his chest.

Allister snorted. "Doctor?"

Drake gestured toward the club. "The guy in the purple suit. He looks exactly like I'd think a witch doctor would look like." He rubbed his chin with a thoughtful look. "Though, I would think he'd have more bones for decorations or perhaps a piercing through his nose." He pointed at his own nose to show his brother.

"You're so weird." Allister sighed and turned to me. "What did Tuma want?"

I shook my head. "Nothing of importance. Though, I had the impression that he thought I should hand Piper over and be done with it. He went so far as to call her simple."

Everyone laughed as I knew they would.

I peeked into the car and looked over Piper's sleeping form. "What shall we do about Piper?"

"I suggest we take this discussion inside." Marcus held the door open. "We do not know who might be listening." His gaze slid over to the two large guards standing nearby.

Nodding, I entered the vehicle. I sat next to Piper, placing her head in my lap. I picked at a piece of her hair that had stuck to her face by Morpheus's leftovers. "We should probably wait until we arrive home. Darren will want to hear about this."

Rayne groaned, holding onto Piper's legs laid across his lap. "Great. He's going to be a big drama queen about it all."

"Especially since the council seemed to not know anything about Piper's relationship with him." Allister stroked his jaw and peered down Piper's unconscious form. "I wonder if Caleb suppressed her relationship with him as well?"

As the car began moving, I stared down at Piper wondering how we'd get through the next few months without her. "I suppose we'll find out soon."

CHAPTER 10

Darren

GRETCHEN TURNED FROM THE sink with a huff. "Would you stop pacing? You're giving me palpitations."

I paused mid stride. "I'm sorry, Gretchen. I don't mean to cause you undue stress." I slid on to the stool at the island. "I just feel as if they should be back by now."

"They will be back when they get back," Gretchen replied stiffly, stirring the sauce on the stove. "Besides, if Antoine dies you'll surely be the first to know."

I snorted. "Thanks. That's really comforting."

Gretchen gave me a sympathetic smile, putting her spoon down long enough to reach across the island to pat my hand. "I understand how you feel Darren, but worrying yourself sick is not going to make them come back faster." She turned back to the stove and picked up her spoon once more before adding, "I just hope that slimy piece of filth gets what's coming to him."

"You and me both," I muttered, leaning on my elbow. I stared down at the counter, stroking my gloved fingers along the top of the surface. I frowned. There was a smudge. We couldn't have that.

I jumped up from my seat dead set on getting a sponge and cleaning supplies when the front door opened.

"They're back!" Gretchen dropped her spoon, not caring that it fell on the floor as she made a dash for the kitchen door. I rushed after her, the smudge on the counter completely forgotten in my need to see how Piper and the others were doing.

The twins came in first. Gretchen rushed over to them, feathering about like a mother hen. When she saw that they were indeed fine, she moved onto Marcus who had some blood splatter on him.

"Oh god, where are you hurt?" Gretchen cried searching for his injury.

Marcus patted her on the shoulder. "Do not fret so. It is not my blood."

Gretchen sighed, clasping her hand to her chest. "Thank goodness. Where's Piper?"

"She's coming," Wynn told her on the way in, his own shirt splattered with blood as well. This did not look good.

I stayed back from the door giving them room to enter. The twins headed straight for the kitchen while Marcus waited in the doorway. Wynn inclined his head toward me on his way up the stairs, not overly concerned it seemed for Piper's safety. It made me feel better and worse at the same time.

Antoine came next.

It took everything in me not to run to him. I wanted to strip him down and search every inch of him for anything that the council might have done. I resisted for the sake of the others, not wanting them to see how worried I had been. I didn't have to pretend with Antoine. He could feel my anxiety which at times was a blessing and a curse.

Today, it was a necessity.

Pulling his jacket off, Antoine approached me holding the jacket out for me to take. It too had blood splatter on it as well as a few places on his face and neck. I frowned after closer inspection seeing some kind of thick meat substance caught on his collar.

I picked it up with my gloved hands and stared at it.

"It's not any of ours," Antoine answered my unasked question. "Well, none of any of us that matter."

My brow arched. "I am to assume this belongs to Morpheus?"

"Morpheus is dead?" Gretchen asked, completely forgetting about the others to hear the news.

"And about damn time," Rayne snapped, bumping the door with his shoulder as he came in carrying an unconscious Piper. "None of you wanted to help huh?"

Gretchen gasped. "What happened to Piper?"

"She's fine," Rayne explained, shifting Piper in his arms. "Just asleep." At that very moment, Piper let out a loud snort. "See, just fine."

"Then why is she covered in blood?" Gretchen asked not letting Rayne pass until she looked him and Piper over completely.

"Let's just say we were in the splash zone." Drake walked back into the foyer, a blood container in his hand.

Gretchen's brows furrowed. "Splash...zone?" Then she seemed to realize there was one person less than who left the house. "You mean, this is all from Morpheus?"

"Yep," Drake popped, sipping from the container. "They blasted his head open like a watermelon." He snapped the fingers on his free hand. "Just like that. We didn't even see it coming." He gestured down at his blood stained shirt.

Approaching Rayne, I peered down at the woman who had changed all our lives. "Why is Piper passed out then?"

Rayne's nose wrinkled and shifted as if there were something he didn't want to tell me. "It's complicated. I'm not even sure I understand it."

"What's to understand?" Drake snorted, coming up beside us. He flicked a piece of Piper's hair and said, "Piper has gotten us all into a weird bind again."

"The council didn't believe we could all be in love with the same woman," Marcus explained with a gruff tone.

"So, how does that have anything to do with it?" Gretchen interjected, her anxiety beginning to rub off on me.

"The short of it is, we're being used as their personal dolls." Rayne sighed and pushed through us to get to the stairs. "Piper's memories of all of us have been suppressed and it will be like she has just started her job here. Or at least...that's what we think?"

"Darren," Antoine called for me. "We need you to move all of Piper's things back to her room. Make sure to check the other rooms for anything that may belong to her. We don't want to make this any more hard than it has to be."

"Of course," I answered without thinking and then paused to add on, "What are the terms of this...experiment?"

Drake leaned against the stair railing and gestured up the stairs. "Piper has six months to fall in love with all of us again, proving that we love her by our own choice and not because of some weird twist of fate or whatever nonsense they were spouting."

My mouth dropped open. How in the...what?

"Yep," Rayne said from the top of the stairs. "That's exactly what we were thinking."

Forgetting propriety for the moment, I turned on Antoine. "Why would you allow this?"

Antoine rolled up his sleeves and let out a long breath. A lot of emotion came with that one single sigh. "We did not particularly have a choice in the matter. The council has to punish us and this is their way of doing so."

"I don't understand." Gretchen clasped her hands together in front of her. "They're making you fall in love again to punish you? How is that a punishment? I would love to fall in love with my husband again."

"Yes, in retrospect it does seem like a good deal. However," Antoine trailed off, tucking his hands into his pockets. "Some things may have moved faster with Piper because we were in danger. I'm not sure we can all woo her in the time limits they have given us."

"And you can't interfere," Allister said from the doorway.

I glanced between them, my frown growing deeper. "What do you mean I can't interfere?"

Antoine sighed again. "She has to fall in love with the six of us. You were not included in those conditions."

"So, you're saying that I have to pretend that Piper and I have no relationship whatsoever while watching the rest of you do everything with her?" I couldn't hold back the anger in my voice. This was ridiculous. How could they possibly think this is a good idea? What if Piper gets her memories back? What if it doesn't work? What if the hunters come searching for her before the end of the six months because fuck knows Vincent is not the patient type.

"Those are all good questions." Rayne said coming down the stairs. "I changed Piper into her night clothes and cleaned the blood off as best I could. I didn't think trying to shower her was a good idea. Especially since she might freak out if she wakes up naked in the shower with her boss."

"Yeah, probably a good idea." Drake bobbed his head. "And what's a good question?"

Rayne stopped in the middle of us. "What do we do if the hunters show up for Piper? It's not like they're going to just wait around for six months?"

"We will deal with that when we come to it," Antoine explained, placing a hand on my arm. The public touching showed me how concerned he actually was about the whole thing. "Right now we can only handle one crisis at a time. Let's get Piper's stuff settled and go to bed." He ushered the others toward the basement.

When it was only Gretchen and me, Antoine gestured for us to follow him into the kitchen. "Just like the first day of Piper working here, I will expect you two to help her through this."

I gritted my teeth. "Of course, master."

Antoine shot me a look before continuing. "We should assume she doesn't know any of us are vampires as before. So we will have to play it by ear as far as having her learn our true identity. I don't expect this to be an easy time for any of us and we need to pull together and get through this." Antoine said this to me with a meaningful look. "We have been through worse. This will not break us."

As I tossed and turned in my bed later that night, unable to sleep without Piper by my side, I wondered how this would affect us. How would this change us for the future? And would we even survive it?

CHAPTER 11

Antoine

SEVERAL HOURS LATER I sat behind my desk on the phone with my accountant.

"I don't know how..." Larry stammered. "All your funds just became unfrozen without a rhyme or reason. No one seems to know why they were frozen in the first place. They are chalking it up to a system glitch."

"I see," I hummed into the phone. "And the properties?"

The shuffling of papers and clacking of keys on a keyboard filled the end of the phone. "Well, you see..." Larry continued, tripping over his words even more than before. "At the current moment all purchases have been put in a standstill. We aren't able to purchase them but they aren't moving forward with the others either. Almost like they are waiting for something."

Not surprising there. Of course I did not relay my thoughts to Larry], he wouldn't understand what was going on. The council had seen fit to give us our money back which was a blessing itself. The hold on my company purchases was another matter. What were they waiting for? Piper to fail? For us to give them some reason to punish us further?

Tuma had me under the impression that they would not want to destroy our family if they did not have to. I would make damn sure that we did not give them a reason to do more harm.

"I will continue to monitor the situation for you, Mr. Durand. And of course I am at your beck and call. Any time of day. Day or night. I'll be here."

I sighed, already tired of the conversation. "Very well, Larry. I will follow up with you at a later date. Let me know if any new occurrences arise." I hung the phone up as Larry continued to blather on. Before I could turn back to the other issues before me a stutter of anxiety in my chest had me glancing up at the closed office door. I could feel Darren standing there. His anxiety and indecision rampaging.

"You might as well come in. Neither of us will get to sleep otherwise," I called out to him loud enough his enhanced hearing could receive it.

The office door opened. Darren stepped inside and promptly closed it behind him. His suit jacket was missing and his necktie was untied, the first few buttons if his shirt undone. He'd also taken his gloves off and his usually perfectly slicked back hair was a mess as if he'd been running his fingers through it.

"What is it?" I leaned back in my chair and laced my fingers in my lap waiting for him to answer. Though, I had an idea of what he had come to see me about.

Darren walked the short length to my desk and braced his hands on the front of it, all professional appearances gone. "You cannot be serious about letting this happen, can you?"

My lips pursed for a moment. "I'm not sure I know what you mean. I didn't let anything happen. We didn't have much of a choice."

"There's always a choice," Darren snapped. "You're one of the strongest vampires around and you let them do this to her? Violate her memories all for some...some game?" He threw his hands up in the air and turned his back on me, pacing the length of my desk.

"While I admit I did urge her to go along with the council's game in hopes that it would help us in the long run, I can assure you nothing was done without Piper's permission." I leaned forward and placed a hand on my desk, my gaze set on Darren's face. "She agreed to this."

"But what of the repercussions? She's going to wake up and find out she has supernatural abilities and freak out."

I held a hand up. "Taken care of. They suppressed her abilities as well as her bond to me so that there would be no unfairness during the trial."

Darren shook his head and laughed, not a happy one. "You know this is completely nuts, right? The Piper of today is not the same one who came through those doors two years ago. How do you even know you'll get her to fall for you again? We'd be lucky if we could even get Wynn to get her, let alone the six of you." He huffed and crossed his arms. His frustration was written all over his face. "And I'm just supposed to sit back and watch as the woman I love falls in love again and again." He drew a hand over his face. "How can you ask this of me?"

I stood and walked around the desk, stopping before Darren to wrap him in my arms. In general, I was not a comforting person, not in life and certainly not in death but I knew when my loved ones needed more. This was definitely a moment where more was the answer.

Darren leaned into my embrace, his face burying in the crook of my neck. His hot breath sprayed across my skin as he spoke.

"I'm not sure I can do this. Of all the things I've done for you, this is the one thing I don't think I can do."

I held him close, a reassuring hand through his hair. "Do not think of it as for me. Do it for Piper. Remember how she was those first few days? She will need you. More than ever before. And when this is all over..."

"If you mean," he added.

I lifted his head with both my hands staring into his eyes. "When this is all over we will be stronger for it. I promise."

Darren stared at me for a long moment, the anxiety in his chest still there but not as aggressive as before.

We stood there together a moment longer before Darren was the one to step away. "What about the hunters? Have you thought of anything to tell them?"

"There is not much we can do about it. We will have to figure out some way to dissuade the hunters from speaking to her until we have finished this trial." I shifted over to the desk and leaned against it, tucking my hands into my pockets. "However, we could just solve the problem with a simple call to Vincent telling him where the council is..."

"But then Piper might be stuck this way."

I nodded. "True. I wish I had all the answers but I am as much in the dark as the rest of you."

Darren's expression darkened. I wished there was more I could do to reassure him. However, I was speaking the truth. I did not know what we should do next. All we could do was handle things as they came. Whichever way that may be.

Head bowed, Darren moved toward the door. I grabbed his arm, stopping him in his tracks.

There was one thing I could do for him.

Darren lifted his gaze to me, an expectant look in his eyes.

I pulled him close and grasped the back of his neck, my fingers tugging at the strands of his black hair. Darren's eyes widened and then his body relaxed against mine.

"That's it," I soothed, allowing my free hand to wander down his body to cup him over his pants. "We both need this tonight."

Darren inclined his head. "Of course, master."

I jerked his head back, stretching out the line of his neck. "You will speak when spoken to."

Darren said nothing. He knew the game well.

"Well?"

Eyes down, Darren answered, "Yes, master."

"Good." I released his head abruptly. "Remove my clothing."

Without a word, Darren reached for my tie, undoing the knot and pulling it loose. He laid it across the chair next to us making sure it was smoothed out before continuing. I had already removed my jacket so he only had my shirt to remove now. I watched Darren closely as he undid each button with precise movements.

I could undress myself. We both knew it. Sometimes it wasn't about what one could do or couldn't. It was about control. Giving up your control to someone else so you did not have to think for a moment. It was especially important when your mind and body was so full of emotion that you could not find an outlet for it. That was all this was. A release we both needed because where else would we get it?

When Darren had me fully unclothed, I waited without a word while he finished folding them on the chair. He then turned to me waiting for my next order.

"Kneel."

Darren silently dropped to his knees, placing his hands on his lap, his eyes down on the ground.

"Look at me."

His gaze lifted from the floor and locked with mine. I brushed a hand over his hair and cupped his chin, tracing a finger over his lips until he opened his mouth. I dipped my finger into his mouth, touching the line of his teeth before removing it. Darren let me do all this without protest, his face a doll-like calm I hadn't seen on him in quite a while. I supposed Piper had something to do with that. She had changed all of us it seemed. Whether we knew it or not.

"Touch me," I ordered not telling him precisely where. Darren didn't need to be told though, he knew exactly what I wanted and where. After all these years, it was easy for us. Like a play we had seen a hundred times. It never got old.

As Darren's hand stroked my length and then cupped my testicles, I let out a grunt of encouragement. His grip grew firmer, his strokes more sure of themselves. Each stroke of my length and his hand quickened until I gripped the back of his head with a gasp, "Stop."

Darren's hand stilled instantly.

"Open your mouth."

Darren complied, leaning into it as I brought my cock toward his face. My hand stayed in his hair as he took me in between his lips, suctioning his cheeks around me. I sighed into the feeling, knowing only one other person who could make me feel this way. I wanted her here now with us. It wasn't fair that she was the one who had to suffer every time. She was the one who always paid the price for us.

With each thought, I thrust myself into Darren's mouth. He took it all without complaint though his eyes watered at some point. When I saw, I eased up, forcing myself to slow down or risk hurting him. My mind wouldn't calm. All I could think about was

Piper and how this would affect her. Perhaps, Darren was right and I hadn't thought this through before letting her volunteer once more to save us.

"Stop," I gasped, jerking myself away from Darren. I sank onto the chair, crinkling my clothing as I did. Darren stared up at me not questioning my sudden actions.

I grasped both arms of the chair and stared out the office window at the night sky. How had it all come to this? Was I even worthy of leading this family any more?

After a long moment, I turned back to Darren and said, "I'm sorry. I'm sorry for it all."

CHAPTER 12
Piper

MY MIND WAS A collage of horror movie images. Or at least that's the only way I could explain them. Blood and gore splattered every part of my mind mixed in with groans and naked bodies. It seemed like my body was confused on if it should be turned on or terrified. The nightmare - dream? - finally stopped when I hit the ground with a hard thud.

Groaning, I grabbed my head and tried to sit up. I found my arms and legs trapped in the sheets. I fought against the sheets, jerking and pulling until I finally could see the light. Or the dim light of day because my curtains were drawn. I frowned and blinked at the room.

Where the hell was I?

It seemed vaguely familiar like I should know where I was but for some ungodly reason I had forgotten.

The room was nice at least. So, whoever kidnapped me had good taste. I crawled off the floor and something occurred to me. Where were my clothes? I patted myself down and realized I was indeed wearing clothes - not ones I even remotely remember buying but clothes nonetheless. I let out a long sigh. That was a relief.

Peering around the room, I found a dresser. Lips twisted to one side, I walked over to it and pulled open the first drawer. Okay, these I recognize. I thought to myself as I pulled a pair of night shorts out. Then my brow furrowed at all the lingerie I did not remember buying. When have I ever worn lingerie...ever?

Not that I was against it, just usually my boyfriends didn't last long enough for me to even bother with buying any. And any one night stand was not worth the effort.

Tossing a pair of panties back into the drawer, I turned to the closet next. There were several normal outfits that I'd seen before and then some not so normal ones. Where did all this leather come from?

I picked up a pair of knee high boots. Was there a costume party I wasn't aware of? I dropped them back in the closet and one fell over. "Oops," I giggled about to ignore it when something came rolling out of the top of the boot.

Frowning, I picked up the small glass vial. Full to the brim with dark red liquid, it took me a second to realize what it was and when I did I almost dropped the thing. Clutching it close to my chest, I scanned the room as if someone had been watching, my heart nearly beating out of my chest.

Blood! What was a vial of blood doing in my boots?

Before I could contemplate any further, a knock on my door had me nearly throwing myself across the room. I shoved the vial back into the top of the boot and shut the closet door with a slam. Hurrying to the bedroom door, I almost opened it without answering. Realizing how dangerous that was, I cleared my throat to ask, "Who is it?"

The answering voice had a very nice tone to it though a bit short. "Darren. The butler."

I frowned. The butler? What butler? Realizing I could probably open the door, I wretched it open with a sheepish grin. "Uh, hi. Darren. Um...sorry I'm having a little hard time remembering where I am...could you?" I waved a finger around the doorway like it would explain everything.

For a long moment, Darren stared at me. So I stared right back and what a hottie he was. Jet black hair that had that slicked back look that gave him a prim and proper- I'd be the best sex you've ever had once you get me off work- look to it. His suit was pressed and not a piece out of place. The only thing was the white gloves he wore on his hands as he handed me a piece of paper.

"You are in the Durand household. You were accepted as the new live-in maid yesterday. This is a list of chores you will be expected to do. I will provide you with a new list daily." He kept talking even as I looked over the list. "The masters are asleep at the moment so I would suggest starting with some of the house cleaning over things such as bathrooms and laundry."

"Got it," I murmured as I chewed on my nail. "Uh…Darren?'

"Yes?" Darren arched a brow and for a second it seemed like he wanted to say something else but then didn't.

"There's a lot of clothes in here I don't remember buying." I gestured at my pajamas. "And I certainly don't remember getting dressed for bed."

Darren sighed as if I were irritating him already. "You must have put them on yourself because I know I certainly didn't and if not, then who? Perhaps you were tired after yesterday's events?" He seemed to really want me to believe the answers provided to me either because he didn't want to talk to me any more or something. I was betting on the former. He seemed like he had a stick up his ass that needed to be pulled out. Too bad he was too much of a bore or I'd be happy to help him.

"And the clothes?" I asked again.

"Most likely from the former maid. Some don't bother taking all their belongings when they leave. So, just think of it as a finders keepers type of situation." Darren placed his hands behind his back. "Now, if that will be all?"

I opened my mouth to ask another question but Darren had already turned and walked away.

"Well, screw you too buddy," I muttered, closing the door.

Turning back to my room, I sat the list of chores on the nearby table. There were two chairs at the small dinette table and for a moment I had a weird sensation of deja vu like I'd seen it somewhere before. I shook my head and laughed it off. Like Darren had said, I saw it last night. I was just too tired to remember it.

Okay, what to wear today?

I did remember coming to the Durands for a live-in maid position. The agency had given me one last chance or I'd be tough out of luck. This was it so I had to make it work. If I got fired, I'd be living in my car again or god help me...I shuddered...living with my parents.

I grabbed a pair of jeans and a t-shirt since there wasn't any kind of dress code given and set about getting ready for work. In the bathroom, I did the essentials and pulled my hair up into a ponytail. Opening the cabinet mirror above the sink, I searched for my toothpaste. Finding it, I went to close the cabinet door and then stopped. Curiously, I opened it back up and stared at the contents inside. It had all the normal things that a medicine cabinet would have: band aids, cotton balls, tampons. What was different about this one was the rack of vials just like the one in the boot early just sitting there like it was just a normal thing to have in the cabinet. Trying not to think about it too much, I closed the cabinet and returned to getting ready for work.

While I brushed my teeth, I decided I'd just ask Darren about the previous maid. Whoever it was must have had real problems. The lingerie, the leather, the vials of blood. What were they? Some kind of a vampire chick from the eighties?

Chuckling to myself, I spit and rinsed, setting my toothbrush back in the holder. Or at least, I thought it was mine. I stared at it for a long moment and then grimaced. I threw it in the garbage. Better safe than sorry.

Grabbing the chores list, I folded it and stuck it in the back pocket of my jeans before heading out the door. I stepped into the hallway and glanced right and left, realizing I had no idea where I was going.

Clicking my fingers and shifting in place, I darted back and forth with which way to go. "Just pick a way. That's it. You can go from there. Just pick one. It's not that hard."

Suddenly a burst of laughter came from the end of the hall making the decision for me. I turned right. A short walk down the hallway led me to a staircase where the laughter was coming from. Hurrying down the stairs, I found myself in the kitchen. Darren sat at the island with a coffee cup in hand while a plump older woman chatted with him.

When I entered, they both stopped talking. Darren didn't move but the older woman turned to greet me. "You must be Piper! Good morning. I'm Gretchen the house cook. How did you sleep?" She came around the island and went in for a hug. I let her because well, I don't really know why. It just seemed the right thing to do. It didn't feel awkward. It was almost like hugging one's grandmother - well not mine, since she was the biggest tight ass I'd ever known.

I patted Gretchen on the back, not sure what to do with my hands until she let me go. I let out a nervous chuckle. "Hi, everyone sure is friendly huh?" I shot a not so subtle look at Darren.

"Oh, don't let that old grouch get you down," Gretchen winked, leading me over to the island. "You just have to know how to work Darren. You'll be fast friends before you know."

Hesitantly I took a seat at the island and gratefully took the cup of coffee Gretchen offered. Before I could ask for it, the plate of cream and sugar already pushed my way. I glanced up and met Darren's gaze. "Uh, thanks."

Darren inclined his head, returning to his coffee.

"So..." I drew out. "What's the Durands like? I mean, they can't be too uptight since they sleep past eight." I laughed but no one laughed with me.

"Oh don't worry about them. They're night owls." Gretchen offered me a small smile as she placed a plate of eggs and toast in front of me. My go-to breakfast most mornings. "You probably won't see them until this evening."

I nodded my head in understanding though I didn't understand at all. How could they afford such a big place and servants for that matter and stay up all night? Didn't they have jobs?

I wanted to ask but didn't think it was proper to ask just yet. At least, not on my first day. It seemed like a second day question.

When I was done eating, I pulled my list out and scanned over it. "Dust the vases." I pushed out of my chair and stood. "Okay, I can do that."

Darren stood abruptly and took the list from my hand.

"Hey!" I tried to grab it.

"Actually, best to stay away from the breakables," Darren said out of the blue, he gave Gretchen a look that made the older woman giggle. "I'll handle that."

"Hey, I'm not going to break anything," I scowled, snatching the list back from him. "I'll have you know I am as graceful as a swan."

Darren's lips curled at one edge and I swear I almost swooned on the spot. "Oh, you are?"

"Y...yes," I stuttered suddenly at a loss for words.

"Well, then I suppose we'll just have to see won't we." Darren turned and walked away. "Try not to break anything too valuable. We wouldn't want you to be indebted to the Durands forever."

I stuck my tongue out after him before turning back to Gretchen. "Geez, is he always such a dick?"

Gretchen just grinned.

CHAPTER 13

Marcus

DOWN IN THE BASEMENT, I couldn't sleep. I laid on my bed and stared up at the ceiling, listening to Piper move around upstairs. She had a distinct foot fall that was hard to miss, especially when she kept humming to herself as she passed above us.

"I guess I'm not the only one having a hard time sleeping," Rayne said from his bed, before a squeak of springs signaled he'd sat up.

"Who could sleep?" Drake remarked with a groan and a sigh. "I'm too worried about how she's going to react to all this."

Allister snorted. "She seems fine enough."

Rayne made a loud moaning sound as he stretched and stood. "That's because she hasn't met any of us yet. Right now all she's thinking about is how much of a dick Darren is and why the previous maid had so much leather." He snickered at that.

"Should we really be leaving here up there with only Darren to oversee her?" Allister asked just as something crashed and then Piper shouted out, "I got it!"

I winced. "I fear more for the fine china than I do for Darren."

Drake chuckled, getting out of his bed as well. "So, how are we going to do this?"

"Do what?" I sat up in my bed, sleep no longer an option.

Shrugging, Drake crossed his arms over his chest. "You know, this make her fall in love with you thing. I mean," he paused and gestured around the room. "Out of all of us, you're the one who needs the most time. I mean, we've already done it once."

My eyebrows rose. "And you think I will have a harder time achieving this goal?"

"Well, we already love her..." Allister began leaving the question open for me.

"And you think I don't?" I stared at the twins with a frown. Sure, I wasn't the most open vampire. I didn't quote poetry or use my body to show that I am interested in someone. That didn't mean that I didn't care.

"Well," Drake hopped up on the side of the couch. "If you do it'll be easier than if you don't."

Allister picked up a football from somewhere and tossed it across the room to his brother. "Because if you do, then you'll actually care about making her happy. If you don't then...well..."

Rayne stepped between the line of the ball throwing, cutting it off before it could go back to Allister. "What he means is that if you love her you'll already know all the little things that will make her happy and that will lead her to falling in love with you."

I frowned. "I know how to make a woman fall for me. I have done it many times."

"Since when?" Drake countered with a smirk. "This isn't the crusades. You can't compliment her on her needle point or whatever it is women did in those days. Piper isn't exactly the refined type." He chuckled and then tried to take the ball back from Rayne which ended up with the three of them wrestling on the floor.

"Do you three mind?" Wynn groaned from his place, sliding his silk clad legs out of his bed. "Some of us are trying to sleep."

Drake finally got the ball and hopped to his feet. "Sorry, just nerves you know."

Wynn nodded, dragging a hand through his unruly black hair. "I understand. We are all under a lot of pressure right now. However, being overtired is not the way to handle this. You will lose your grip on your hunger once it comes time for Piper's cycles and then where will we be? With one frightened maid screaming for the authorities. Then this will have been all for nothing."

"Geez, I get it. Fine." Drake tossed the ball toward the couch and then collapsed on his bed. "I'll go to sleep."

"Yeah, me too." Allister laid down on his own bed but neither one of them closed their eyes. They simply stared at the ceiling as we had been doing before.

Rayne did not go back to sleep. He walked over to my bed and sat down at the end. "Look, Piper's not that complicated. You two already have an attraction to one another. I've seen it. She wants you. And I know she cares about you. So what was stopping you two from getting together before all this?"

I stared down at my hands not answering him.

"Ahhh," Rayne bobbed his head. "I get it."

"You shouldn't read others' private thoughts," I chastised him, scowling. Though I complained it was nice not having to voice my issues.

Rayne inched closer to me and clapped me on the back. "Look, don't focus so much on what's not there. Focus on what is there. You don't have to be like the rest of us. You're you and that's all that matters. It isn't about what you can give her that we can't. Believe me, I'm not comparing myself to that sex maniac over there." Rayne gestured toward Wynn who sniffed and laid back down on his bed, his eyes too going to the ceiling.

"So your advice is…" I trailed off, pursing my lips.

"Be yourself," Rayne reiterated, patting me on the shoulder. "The rest will come. Don't worry so much. Women don't require as much as they used to back in your day. A little romance here, a compliment there. Just let her know you're interested without being a dick about it."

I arched a brow, glancing in the direction of Antoine's empty bed.

Rayne threw his head back and laughed. "Okay, so the dick thing works for some guys. Antoine is a special kind of dick. Don't try to be him. Just be you and it will be fine."

"Alright," I nodded and stood.

Rayne frowned. "Where are you going?"

I paused at the basement stairs. "To greet the new maid? After all, you did say I would need the longest time. I might as well start now."

The others didn't protest as I made my way up the stairs. I wasn't sure about what Rayne said. The women when I was alive were very insipid creatures. Their heads full of babies and petty things. Most of them weren't educated the way the women of today were. Their male family members taking care of everything for them, including marriage. I'd been too busy fighting a war to worry about marriage yet. Since then I had only used women for a passing feed or fuck. Piper could be neither of those.

Antoine stopped me at the top of the stairs. "Going somewhere?"

I shifted so that he could pass. "To go introduce myself to Piper…again."

Humming, Antoine inclined his head. "That's a good idea. She's in the foyer right now, cleaning up the Carnets D'Equateur she broke. I snuck down before she could see me. I do not think it is a good idea for her first meeting to be with me."

I agreed but not for the reasons Antoine might think. He may think he's the hard ass everyone thinks he was but really he cared too much and didn't know how to show it. Look at us, there wouldn't be a house of Durand if not for Antoine saving us. So if anything, Antoine needed to be last just so he could get himself together long enough to not screw it all up by making Caleb give her memories back.

"Goodnight," I tossed over my shoulder as I walked into the dining room and barely just missing Piper with her hands full.

"Oh my holy ball sacks!" She cried out, throwing the dust pan full of glass pieces into the air. I grabbed her around the waist and jerked her out of the way of the falling debris. With her pressed firmly against my body it was hard to remember that she didn't know who I was anymore and that this wasn't entirely appropriate. Though, the hitch in her scent told me that she wasn't totally unhappy to be there.

Reluctantly, I set her down and stepped back. "My apologies. I did not mean to frighten you."

"It's okay." Piper swallowed, her eyes scanning over me unabashedly. "I'm Piper, by the way. I don't think we've met..." She then squinted at me. "Or have we?"

My lips ticked up. "No, we haven't. I'm Marcus."

"So...do you work here as well?" She twisted her pony tail between her fingers, pulling her lower lip between her teeth.

Before I could answer, Darren appeared with a broom and a trash can. "Oh, Master Durand, excuse me."

Piper's eyes widened and her entire demeanor changed. She dropped her hands and looked from side to side before kneeling on the ground. Piper began grabbing pieces of glass without paying any mind to what she was doing which only figured the next thing would happen.

"Ouch, fuck." Piper hissed, lifting her hand up. A slice across her finger dripped with blood.

I knelt before her and took her hand. "Let me see. It's not too deep." I could feel her gaze on me as I looked over her finger. I thought about what I should do in that moment. The vampire in me wanted to lick the blood off her finger. If Piper had her memories, I probably would have. As it were...

I cleared my throat and stood. "Darren please see to it that Piper finds a bandage." I nodded to both of them and abruptly walked into the kitchen.

What the hell is wrong with me?

CHAPTER 14
Piper

WHAT THE HELL? THAT was one of the Durands? Why did my first impression have to be of a drooling school girl? I mean could I have been any more slutty?

"So that was Marcus?" I tried to be casual about it as I cleaned up the broken glass after having bandaged my finger.

Darren held the trash can out for me. "Yes, one of the six members of the Durand family."

I swallowed. "Ah, so there's six of them. Gotcha. Are they all so..." I waved the dust pan in the air. "Hot as hell?"

Darren stared at me for a long moment.

"What?" I gaped at him. "I have eyes. I'm not going to pretend they don't exist just because I work for them."

Shaking his head, Darren sat the trash can down. "Listen, Piper. Do your job and try not to break anything. That's all that matters. As far as I'm concerned, the Durands could look like a pack of rats. It would not change how I do my job and nor should it affect yours."

I bobbed my head. "Yeah, got it. Do my job. Thanks." I continued to clean up the mess, my mind wondering what the other Durands would look like. If they looked anything like Marcus or Darren did then I was going to be in very big trouble.

"How long have you worked for the Durands?" I dumped the dust pan full of glass pieces into the trash can.

Darren glanced off to the side. "I've been with the Durands for as long as I can remember. Gretchen as well. And if you're lucky..." he turned his gaze onto me, an intense look in his eyes, "You'll be with us for a long time."

"Uh…" My eyes darted from one side to the other trying to look anywhere but at Darren. The guy might be hot as fuck but he was creepy as all get out. "Alright, well, I'm going to go take my lunch break and then get to work on the laundry. So…yeah." I walked away not making eye contact with him the whole way out.

I kind of hoped that Marcus would be in the kitchen when I arrived. Sadly, it was only Gretchen. She was nice enough and knew how to make some good eggs. However, she wasn't a tall stoic guy with biceps for days and eyes that would have you drowning in the deep dark orbs.

"Piper," Gretchen greeted me as I came in. "How has your morning been?"

I sat down at the island and laced my fingers on the counter. "Alright, I did break a few things. Cut my finger." I held up said finger. "And drooled all over one of the bosses."

Gretchen chuckled. "Well, I don't blame you. If I didn't see them as one of my own I wouldn't have minded taking a tumble or two with the twins."

My brows shot to my hair line. "T...twins? There's twins?"

Stepping over to the fridge, Gretchen winked at me as she opened the door. "Don't let yourself get overwhelmed dear. Just take them one at a time. That's how I'd do it. Then...you know...when you're ready you can see if you can handle them all at once." She stared off into the distance and sighed dreamily.

For some reason I felt like she wasn't talking about what I thought she was talking about anymore.

"Anyway," Gretchen snapped out of her daze. "Would you like a sandwich?"

"Oh," I jumped up from my seat. "I can do that. You don't have to make me anything."

"Nonsense." Gretchen waved me off, pulling a few packages from the fridge. "The boys rarely let me cook for them. Always so busy you know," she explained with a knowing look. "It's nice to have another woman around the place."

"Oh?" My brows rose. "Do the Durands not have girlfriends? Boyfriends?" I tried to be casual about it but the smirk on Gretchen's lips told me I didn't do a very good job of it.

Gretchen put together my sandwich with a secretive smile. "No, not that I know of. What do you think, Darren?"

My head turned to the side as Darren stepped into the room and over to the fridge.

"What do I think of what?"

"Are the Durands seeing anyone?" Gretchen repeated her smile no longer held back.

Curiously, Darren's shoulders stiffened at the question. He closed the fridge without getting anything and spun around. His gaze hardened on Gretchen who's grin didn't even flinch at the daggers he was shooting in her direction. Then he promptly walked out the back kitchen door.

Gretchen sat my plate in front of me. I grabbed the sandwich and asked, "What's his problem?"

"Unrequited love," was all she said before turning her back on me.

Taking a big bite of my sandwich, I moaned in pleasure. As I swallowed, I flipped open the top of the bread to see what

Gretchen had put on the sandwich. "Mustard and mayo? How did you know I like both?"

Gretchen shrugged a shoulder. "It's a gift."

"Hey Gretchen, could I get some crackers?"

My head lifted from my heavenly sandwich and almost choked. There standing in the kitchen doorway was the most adorable guy I had ever seen. I didn't use the word adorable lightly. Most guys were hot or handsome. This one was just downright cute and it worked for him. From the top of his ruffled red hair to the bottom of his high top shoes.

The guy crossed his arms over his dark green t-shirt and leaned on the doorway, a little look of concern on his face. "Are you okay?"

I nodded dumbly as Gretchen handed me a glass of water. I swallowed it down quickly only to give myself a coughing fit that had the cutie pie patting me on the back.

"Geez, are you always this eager to die?" The guy chuckled sliding into the seat next to me. "I'm Rayne by the way. Durand."

My eyes widened and I quickly wiped the back of my hand over my mouth. "Uh, hi, Piper. The maid."

Rayne bobbed his head then turned back to Gretchen. "So? Crackers?"

Gretchen placed her hands on both hips and arched a brow. "You know very well where they are. Why don't you get them yourself?"

Rayne groaned. "But you're so much closer."

Shaking her head, Gretchen turned to the cabinet and retrieved the box Rayne requested. "I swear, you may be older but you act worse than my grandchildren."

"Older?" I frowned, glancing between the two. Rayne couldn't be more than a year or two younger than me while Gretchen had to at least be fifty or more.

Rayne coughed, covering his mouth with his hand. "Uh, that's not what she meant."

Gretchen's eyes widened. "Oh, no. I mean he's older than my grandchildren." Her cheeks flushed a pretty shade of pink and she seemed much younger than fifty now.

"Oh okay," I mumbled to myself, returning to my sandwich. Just focus on work and not all the hot guys running around. I could not afford to lose this job because of my libido. This was my last chance damn it.

Rayne chuckled beside me.

I shot a look in his direction, brows furrowed. "What's so funny?"

Rayne shook his head and popped a cracker into his mouth. "Nothing, you just seem like a big overthinker is all."

"I do?" No one has ever called me an overthinker. More like an underachiever. I had always strived to do the most mediocre amount possible. No one wanted to get stuck with more work for being good at their job or get fired for doing too little. A happy middle had always been my place.

This time Rayne snorted and almost choked himself. I slapped him on the back with an even more confusion whirling inside of me. This guy was a weird one.

"Sorry," Rayne cleared his throat. "Just remembered something funny." He picked his box of crackers up and stood from the island. "Thanks for the crackers. Nice to meet you Piper."

I raised a hand in a wave at his retreating back. Then turned back to Gretchen. "The men here sure are weird ones. Hotter than hell, but weird."

Gretchen burst out laughing. "Honey, you don't know the half of it."

CHAPTER 15

Piper

EVENING HAD FINALLY COME and I was
more excited to meet the rest of the Durands
than I had been about going to my first party
in high school. Not that I had gone to many.
I made friends easily. I just wasn't very good
at keeping up with them. I always seemed to
be in my own little world.

Hmmm. Wonder why?

Anyway, I'd finished up all the bathrooms
and started the laundry without running into

any of the other Durands. Which shouldn't have been surprising, I mean the house was huge. I could probably go days without seeing any one but Darren and Gretchen, who had been the only constants in my day. Gretchen there to feed me. Darren there to make a weird but snide comment. I had a feeling Darren just needed to get laid and all that nastiness would go away.

My list of chores were done for the day and it was time to find some dinner. I walked down the main stairs and into the foyer. The house was so neat and clean already I wondered what they even needed me for. Darren seemed more than capable of handling the household himself since he'd basically spent the day following me around and making sure I didn't break anything else.

Kind of annoying really.

Walking into the dining room, my eyebrows shot up. No one was in there. My stride slowed as I tried to listen for some form of life. It was evening right? Shouldn't they be up by now? Rayne and Marcus had shown up earlier today and none of them had been in their bedrooms when I went around and picked up the laundry.

Lips pressed into a thin line, I marched toward the kitchen where I was sure Gretchen would have something scrumptious to eat and hopefully some answers.

"Oh, excuse me there."

I jumped back from the muscular man who seemed to appear out of nowhere. I glanced around, my brows furrowed. "Where did you come from?"

The man stepped aside to point at the door behind him. "The basement."

Feeling a bit dumb, I flushed. "Oh." Then I cocked my head to the side and stared at the door. "Why were you in the basement? I'm Piper by the way. The maid." I offered my hand and then realized how stupid that was and tried to take it back but the man grabbed it before I could.

He had a nice handshake. Not too firm and not too soft. He shook it like he actually respected me and didn't expect me to break just because I was a woman. I mean the guy could probably break me in half with the guns on him. It was nice that he wasn't so full of himself though to make it all his personality.

"Allister," the man introduced himself. "And I was sleeping. We all sleep down there during the day."

I frowned. "Why?"

Allister scratched the back of his neck and glanced off to the side. "Oh you know. It's so noisy up here with the vacuuming and such, it's much quieter down stairs."

I bobbed my head pretending to understand. This house was worth millions there was no way that they could hear the vacuum through the walls. Whatever. Rich people.

"Anyway," I shifted in place, trying to look anywhere but at his massive pecs. "I was just heading to get dinner."

"Oh, go ahead." Allister gestured with his arm, a small smile on his face. Everyone was just so darn charming and accommodating. It was very strange.

Walking into the kitchen, I went to the fridge where the door was open. "Hey what's for dinner? I'm starving."

The door closed revealing Allister, who said with a smirk, "Me too. Wanna help a guy out?"

I jerked back and gaped. "Wait, weren't you just..." I glanced back at the dining room where Allister had been and then the man in front of me. "And now you're..." then I remembered. "Oh, wait you're one of the twins right?"

The not Allister guy leaned on the fridge so his arm was above me. "Yep. That'd be me. I guess you've met Allister already. I'm Drake."

I glanced up and down his flirty frat boy expression and rolled my eyes. "Piper," then I added on, "And if you're looking for me to cook, you're barking up the wrong tree. I'm lucky enough to boil water."

"Well, then maybe I could give you a lesson some time," Drake continued without a break in his whole demeanor. "You know, we could have some dinner. Get to know each other. That kind of thing."

"Oh, really?" I arched a brow, taking a step back from him even further.

"Oh yeah." Drake dropped his arm and followed after me. "I'm all about employee satisfaction. I want to make sure you are a hundred percent happy here."

The words coming out of his mouth didn't quite match the tone he was using. Either he was coming on to me or he was just weird like the rest of them. I wasn't sure which one would make me more comfortable.

"Uh, I think I'll pass for tonight. Thanks anyway." I moved away from him and started for the back stairs, thinking I could just come back and get something later.

Thankfully, Gretchen came to my rescue. She walked in the back door and stated, "Drake get over here and help an old woman out. Use those muscles for something other than flexing in the mirror."

I snorted and paused on the stairs then decided it would be rude to not offer my help as well. I mean, the woman was cooking for me all the time after all.

"Here, let me." I held out my hands to take one of the bags from her as Drake grabbed the others. We had a moment where our eyes locked and it was like a jolt hit me right in the chest. Weirded out by the feeling I was having, I hurried to put the bags on the island before turning on my heel and darting up the stairs.

My steps slowed as Gretchen and Drake began talking. Knowing I was out of sight, I pressed myself against the wall and leaned in, hoping to hear something that might explain all the strangeness going on around this place.

"How do you think it's going?" Gretchen asked.

A chair scraped against the floor and Drake answered, "Hard to tell. She's more suspicious than she was before."

Before? Who were they talking about? Couldn't be me, I'd never met the guy before today.

"Well, you've only got six months to make it work," Gretchen told him, followed by some pots and pans clanging together. "You better get a move on or this will all be for nothing."

Drake groaned. "Don't remind me. This whole thing is a crock of shit. Who in their right minds could fall in love that quickly."

There was a pause before Gretchen said, "You did before remember?"

"What are you doing?"

I jumped in place and nearly fell down the stairs, Darren grabbed a hold of me before I could break my neck. I clung to him and stuttered out, "Thanks."

"You're welcome," Darren replied stiffly before removing himself from me as if I had some kind of cooties. "So what were you doing loitering on the stairs? Not eavesdropping are you?" Darren asked loudly and the talking in the kitchen promptly stopped.

"Uh…no no. I wasn't eavesdropping." I raised my voice and called behind me, "I wasn't eavesdropping." Then turned back to Darren. "Excuse me." I marched up the stairs making sure my shoes stomped hard on each step. When I reached the top of the stairs I found Darren following behind me.

I growled, spinning around to shove a finger at his chest. "Look, I don't know what your problem is but you've been nothing but a dick to me since we met this morning. So why don't you just stay out of my way and I'll stay out of yours okay?"

Darren glanced down at the finger touching him and then back up at me, his expression softening. "I'm sorry. I didn't mean to give you that impression. Please understand that I had no intentions of being a dick to you."

I huffed and crossed my arms. "Well, you could have fooled me."

A little laugh came from Darren. "Yes, well. Let's start over, shall we?" He held his gloved hand out toward me.

I stared at it briefly before grasping it with mine. What the hell? Might as well make my life easier. "Those gloves are weird by the way."

Darren's lips ticked up. "Yes, I know."

Dropping his hand, I walked toward my room once more. Darren didn't follow after me and I was almost to my room before I stopped and thought of something.

"Hey, can I ask you something?" I peered over my shoulder at Darren who waited for me to continue. "The last maid here...was she some kind of vampire goth freak?"

Darren's face expression went flat. "What do you mean?"

I felt like such an idiot. "There's a lot of vials of blood in my room and I just thought maybe the last maid was into some kind of weird shit."

Placing his hands behind his back, Darren inclined his head, amusement twinkling in his eyes. "I suppose you could say that. Good night, Piper."

I watched as he walked back down the stairs, my hand on my door handle as I shook my head. "Weird family. Just so fucking weird."

CHAPTER 16

Antoine

A KNOCK ON MY office door had me glancing up from my phone. "Come in."

The door pushed open and in walked Piper. It was curious to see her this way. Shy and out of her element. She was usually so full of fire that I couldn't say two words to her without getting her riled up.

So, when she walked into my office her eyes flicking around the office before settling on me, I watched with a forced calm. Her pupils dilated slightly and her arousal filled the room. Good to know even without memories she wanted me. It wasn't that much of an achievement to be fair.

"You wanted to see me, sir?"

Damn it. Why did she have to go ahead and call me that now? That's right. This Piper did not know me. Or have much of a backbone...yet.

"Yes, Miss Billings, have a seat please." Her last name felt wrong coming out of my mouth. I wanted to take it back but couldn't.

Piper shot a look at me once more trying to hide that she was checking me out as she sat in the chair before me.

Lounging back in my chair, I surveyed her posture noting every inch of discomfort in her form. There was nothing more than I wanted to do than to put her at ease. However, I was not the one to do so, at least not for this Piper.

"What did you want to see me about, sir?" She crossed one leg over the other and shifted in her chair once and then twice.

"Please, Antoine," I offered her, earning myself a surprised look. I could look at this like I was being punished or I could look at this like an opportunity to try again. Our beginnings were not what I wanted them to be. I was far more closed off to her than I should have been. The other day proved that when I had to practically shout my feelings from the rooftops for everyone to hear.

"Okay...Antoine," Piper edged out and then shifted in her seat again. "You can call me Piper then...I guess."

I offered her a small smile before continuing, "I wanted to see how you were doing? Do you have any questions? Concerns? Anything at all I could be of help with?"

Piper pulled her lower lip between her teeth worrying as she studied me. There was something on her mind. I couldn't feel her emotions anymore but I could still read her tells. She wanted to confide in me but something was holding her back.

"Please talk freely. I won't bite," I gave her a closed mouth grin. "I promise."

The tension in Piper's shoulders dropped a bit and she uncrossed her legs, leaning forward in her chair. "I'm just a little confused about a few things."

"Very well," I placed my hands on my desk and angled toward her. "I will do my best to clear them up for you."

Piper breathed deeply before beginning, "First off, why is there so many clothes from past workers in my room? I mean, they're all my size. So unless you have a specific size and height qualification for this job, that's super weird. Then there's the vials of blood I keep finding hidden all over the place. Like who's blood is it? My blood? Your blood? Is it even human blood? Or is it fake blood for some kind of weekend kink show you guys don't want me to know about?"

I opened my mouth to try and answer her. I didn't get the chance.

"Then there's the basement thing." She stood from her chair and paced back and forth before me. "I mean, it's not too weird to sleep during the day and not at night, a lot of people have third shifts but you're obviously loaded so I'm not exactly sure how that works. I mean, unless you're some kind of international spies or something..." She paused and looked at me. "You're not spies are you?"

I shook my head. "No."

Then she was back to it. "Then there's also the whole sleeping together in the same room down there thing. Like who does that? Are you guys really that close? I mean, none of you look alike. Well, I guess that's not true, the twins look alike obviously, their twins. Of course, they would look like each other. Well, except for Drake has this slight crook in his nose that his brother doesn't and Allister has a more soft disposition than Drake's in your face attitude. Do you know what I mean?"

"Piper."

"Huh?"

I reached out to her with a concerned frown. "Breathe." She pulled in a few deep breaths letting them out just as quickly before sinking back into her chair.

"Sorry. I guess a lot of stuff has just bottled up for me the last couple days. I didn't mean to unload it on you." She spoke with her hands as she tried to apologize for her rambling. "I mean, you're my boss, I shouldn't be complaining to you anyway. You know what," she stood and held her hands up. "Just forget it. Forget I said anything at all."

I called after her before she could get out the door.

"What?" Piper quipped, her hand on the door handle.

Unfortunately, I was unable to get my next words out because the office door opened, forcing Piper to back up. Darren appeared in the doorway. He took one look at Piper and me before locking his gaze with mine. "There's a Mr. Vincent here to see you about that matter..."

Wonderful. I supposed I could be grateful that the president of the vampire hunters had waited this long to come beating down our door for their information. Now I just had to keep Piper away from him.

Standing, I buttoned the front of my jacket and ushered Piper out of the office. "Why don't you take the rest of the day off? I have an important client to meet with and we can continue this later." I placed a hand on her shoulder and peered down at her. "Please do not hesitate to come to me with any problems. Anything at all, okay?"

Piper nodded her answer and headed down the hallway. When she was out of earshot, Darren turned to me, arching a brow. Ignoring the look he was giving me, I started toward the stairs.

"Do you even know what you're going to say to him?" Darren asked me quietly coming up behind me on the stairs.

I glanced over my shoulder at him. "What do you suggest I say to him? The truth? How would that be beneficial to any of us? No, it would put Piper and the rest of us in danger." I paused at the bottom of the stairs and pivoted to face Darren. "I will handle Vincent. You just make sure that Piper does not have a mental breakdown." I rubbed my chin between my thumb and index finger and sighed, "From the way she was going on in my office I have a feeling it's coming any day now." With that final note, I stalked into the living room where Vincent sat on one of our couches.

When the slimy git saw me, he did not budge an inch. He lifted his cup of tea to his lips. "Well isn't this an interesting surprise? I was expecting to see Piper and instead I got the head of the Durand household." He sat his cup down on the saucer before him as I took the seat across from him. "Now, what do I owe this pleasure?"

Noting the sarcasm in his tone, I forced my body to relax into the chair. "Piper is unavailable at this time. What can I help you with?"

"Ah, now..." Vincent scooched to the end of his seat and stared me down. "See, I was under the impression that I owned your asses and when I say, 'jump,' you say, 'how high?' And when I say I want to see Piper..." he held his hands out before him waiting for me to fill in the blanks.

I kept my eyes locked on his as I spoke. "Piper is under the weather and cannot see you at this point in time. Now, I will ask again, 'what can I help you with or did you just come here to gloat?'"

Wrinkles appeared in Vincent's brow. "Well, I'm sad to hear that Piper is not feeling well. I hope it's nothing serious?"

"I assure you, we have it well in hand." I hoped that would be enough to satisfy him so he would leave.

Sadly, it was not.

"Well, that is good to hear. I would hate to lose my best hunter over something as common as the flu." He shuddered as he stood up, buttoning the gold button of his garish green suit. The lights glinted off the product in his hair as he moved. "I don't want to waste anymore of your precious time. I came for what we agreed upon."

"And what would that be?" I asked even though I knew exactly what he wanted. The man just annoyed me.

"Why, the location of the council of course!" Vincent grinned, throwing his hands up before him. "You all get your freedom and you give me the keys to the kingdom so to speak."

I stood from my chair and walked the short distance to stand before him. "I do not know the location of the council at this point in time. We have not been summoned to them yet. And with Piper under the weather we can all hope that won't change any time soon."

Vincent frowned. "I was under the impression that the council wanted to see you...badly. Why would they wait so long to call you out?"

I peered straight into Vincent's eyes and asked, "Why would I know what the council thinks? I am simply a pawn in their little game just as we are in yours. Now," I stepped back from him and gestured toward the front door. "I will let you know as soon as we find something out. We appreciate your patience in this matter and for stopping by."

Giving me a suspicion once over, Vincent did not question me further. He stalked toward the door, his eyes scanning around him as if we were keeping Piper hidden somewhere.

When he was gone, Wynn appeared behind me. "What did the great hunter want?"

"Piper," I stated and then sighed, sitting back down in my chair. "And the location of the council."

Wynn walked further into the room, a glass of blood in his hand. "And what did you tell him?"

I grunted and looked up at him. "You shouldn't carry that around so nonchalantly with Piper in her condition."

Wynn took a sip of the blood and grimaced. "You know it's just not the same when you've been taking it directly from the source. Not to forget the delectable spice that is added to it while given mid intercourse."

I grunted again in response.

"So..." Wynn sat on the arm of my chair and poked at my face. "What did you tell him?"

I swatted his hand away. "What do you think? That we didn't know and would tell him when we did."

"And Piper?" Wynn slid off the chair's arm and strode across the room before promptly flopping onto the couch. "What did you tell him about her?"

I rubbed my forehead. I could feel a migraine coming on. "That she's sick."

Wynn snorted. "You're lucky the hunters don't know shit about human servants or he would have seen right through that blatant lie. Human servants don't get sick after they've been bonded to a vampire."

I shot him a glare. "I am aware of that little fact, thank you very much. Did you have something useful to add or did you just come in here to annoy me?"

Wynn's lips ticked up at the edges. "Neither. Both. I haven't decided yet."

"I heard you haven't introduced yourself to Piper yet," I countered, leaning on my elbow. "Is there a reason why?"

Circling the blood in his glass, Wynn didn't meet my gaze as he answered, "Anticipation. The longer it takes for her to meet me the more she will think about me. Wonder what I look like. What I sound like. In the end she will come crawling to me." His lips curled up in a wicked grin suddenly. "Which reminds me of this one night, where Piper was being particularly naughty and I took this cord and wrapped it around her..."

"Please stop." I held a hand up. "This is hard enough without visuals."

Wynn snorted. "Like you're one to talk. You have Darren to fill your lonely nights." I settled him with a look. "Or are things not so well in paradise?"

I crossed my leg and turned away from him. "We're both feeling the pressure right now. It's hard to connect when you're too focused on what you don't have."

Wynn hummed and sipped his blood. "Do you ever think it's easier as a human?"

"What?"

"Loving someone."

I shifted in my seat and stared out the window. "I suppose it's a lot less life threatening. Though, it's not something I ever think I'll know."

Wynn sighed. "Pity."

CHAPTER 17

Wynn

THREE DAYS I WAITED for Piper to come to me and...nothing. Absolutely nothing. Not once have I found her asking about me or even coming to sniff by my bedroom door.

In fact, she only seemed interested in Marcus and Rayne. I suppose I couldn't really expect to do better than our first meeting. It really was perfect.

The first day I saw her, sitting there on the couch twiddling her thumbs while she waited for Darren to come back, I didn't know we would be here years later. It was that first stammered hello that drew me in. Of course, part of it was her lovely face and gorgeous body. Not to forget, the delectable scent of her blood when she fell over herself trying to get away from me. However, you wouldn't hear me telling Piper that - at least not now - she wouldn't find it amusing or endearing to hear about me getting hard from the scent of her blood.

In any case, I had finally decided to seek her out. Like an addict, a man can only go so long without getting a hit of his favorite drug and I was having withdrawals.

"I'm telling you, you have to try french fries in ice cream. It will change your life."

I followed the sound of Piper's voice to the kitchen where she sat between Rayne and Marcus as usual. Even the twins had a hard time getting between those two. I didn't know what it was about the two of them, why she found them so compelling now when the first time around she'd hated the first one and barely spoke to the other one.

This should be easier than it is.

"Ah, there he is!" Rayne twisted in his seat at the island to grin at me. "Piper, this is Wynn. The last of the Durands."

Piper's smile stayed plastered on her face as she continued to explain to Marcus how to make her concoction, barely giving me more than a nod in greeting.

Frowning, I went to the fridge and opened the door. Grabbing my metal container, I twisted off the cap, taking a large drink. The cool liquid slid down my throat and barely sated my thirst for Piper. I wanted nothing more than to wrap her up in my arms and never let her go.

"You and me both, Wynn." Rayne clapped me on the shoulder as he rounded the island. "You and me both."

I grimaced and glanced over my shoulder at Piper, giggling at something Marcus had said. Maybe we had all been a little prideful about our relationship with Piper. We took for granted that she would always want us and we wouldn't have to make any effort to keep her. Now, I saw myself unable to break through that barrier the second time around and it hurt.

"So," Piper swiveled in her chair to finally look at me fully, "there's no way all of you are related unless your mother had very different tastes in men." She grinned and openly ogled all three of us.

I licked my lips and sat the container on the counter, leaning over it to meet her gaze. "We are more of an adopted family than blood related."

Piper nodded. "Got it. So, your parents adopted you or you adopted yourselves?" Her brows furrowed, leaning her face on her hand. "How would that work exactly? Can I get adopted into a famous family now if I wanted to? Cause I can tell you I have quite a few of them on my list that I would love to be a part of."

Rayne and Marcus chuckled at her words. I simply watched her. This Piper was so much different than the one that we knew before. So carefree and full of life. No stress of our lives or the hunters pulling her down. Part of me almost wishes that we could keep her this way. That we didn't have to give her memories back just so she could be this happy and free.

A larger, more selfish part of me screamed no way. I could barely go three days without having her in my arms. There was no way I could let her go without a fight. I needed her to look at me the way she was looking at Marcus right now. Like I was the one thing in life she wanted more than anything. I needed to know the smell and taste of her skin under my mouth once more. If I had to give her up, I wasn't sure that I could go on. Eternity seemed like such a long time alone.

"Oh dear God, Wynn," Rayne groaned, bumping me on the shoulder as he walked out of the kitchen.

I frowned and followed after him, unable to handle watching Piper coo over Marcus while I got nothing.

"Man, could you be more morose?" Rayne shook his head and went to the basement door, throwing it open for both of us to descend. "I mean out of all of us you have the most advantage. She fell for you first. Why should this time be any different?"

I stalked down the steps following him into the basement. "Because she is different. This isn't like last time. We didn't have a chance meeting during her interview. There's no mystery or danger in our meeting. A hello over the kitchen counter is not going to win me her affections."

Rayne rolled his eyes at me, flopping down on his bed. "I still think you are being overly dramatic. We've only been at this for a few days. We have half a year to get her to fall for us. It doesn't have to be instantaneous."

I sank down onto the side of my bed. "For me it was."

"Really?" Rayne glanced my way, arching a brow. "You fell for her right away?"

I nodded. "I didn't know it at the time. I just thought she was a clumsy girl I wanted to take a bite out of. I didn't know I'd fall in love with her strange habits of saying whatever was on her mind. Or that clicking thing she does with her tongue when she's nervous."

Rayne stared across the room. "Huh. Who'd figured the sex god himself was the one who was ensnared first."

I snorted. "Do not act so surprised." I threw my legs up on the bed, leaning against the headboard. "I will have you know before I became a vampire and had all these powers at my disposal, I fell in love quite frequently." I stared down at my hands as if I could tangibly hold my gift in my hands. "I had a different woman every week who was the new light of my life. However, back then their husbands or fathers would chase me off because it was improper to have such affairs out of wedlock."

Rayne threw his head back and laughed. "Fucking hell, you were a scoundrel back then as much as you are now. I'm surprised you could even keep it in your pants long enough to devote yourself to Piper."

"Pardon me," I shot a glare his way. "I will have you know that I was completely faithful to all the women I have been with up until I was run off. I have never once looked at another woman once I was set on one."

Rayne inclined his head. "Sorry. I was only joking."

A distinct giggle and then a moan had both of us looking up at the ceiling.

"Huh," Rayne huffed with a laugh. "I guess Marcus is even further ahead of the game than we thought."

CHAPTER 18

Marcus

I WASN'T SURE WHY I brought Piper to the library. Why didn't I just take her back to my room? Maybe because this was where all of our meaningful moments had happened? Like the time she almost fell off the ladder. Though, she seemed to have a habit of falling off things. This time it happened to be right into my arms.

"Where are we going?" Piper giggled holding onto my hand as I led the way. She took one look at the library and her eyes twinkled with mischief. "You're an odd one, you know that?"

"I've been told that." I smirked at her before backing her up against the nearest bookshelf to kiss her. Kissing Piper was like breathing air when I was alive. I didn't need it. I had to have it. If Piper were the sun, then I would gladly stand in its rays and burn.

"I shouldn't be doing this," Piper said into my mouth, her hands going underneath the back of my shirt. "You're my boss."

I pulled away from her mouth and kissed down her cheek to her jaw and then her neck. "Technically, Antoine is your boss. He's the one who pays you. I just reap the benefits."

Piper angled her head to the side for me, letting out a long breathy moan. "Well, I can definitely say I am enjoying the job perks."

She tugged on my shirt, a silent command to take it off. I couldn't tell this woman no. Stripped of my shirt, Piper's hands trailed up my muscles playing along the lines of my abs before tracing the edge of my jeans. I'd never been more hard in my life.

"So...do you take all the maids up to the library to talk?" She teased, her hands playing a game of hide and seek inside my pants.

When her hand wrapped around me, I almost blacked out. It'd been so long since I'd been with a woman I thought that I might not need that part of myself anymore. But standing here with the most beautiful woman in the world, her tiny hand playing up and down my length and I know I was wrong. So very wrong.

I gasped and braced my hands on the shelf behind her, leaning down so I could capture those tempting lips once more.

A part of me couldn't believe this was happening. That I finally was going to be able to show Piper how much I cared for her. The other part of me was worried that this was moving too fast. Maybe she wouldn't see me as partner material? Maybe this would be just a one time fling? Then I remembered Piper didn't do that. She had never once showed me or any of the others that all she wanted was sex. I was sure she could get anywhere easily if she wanted to. No, Piper was in for the long haul.

"Where's your head?" Piper asked out of the blue.

"What?" I opened my eyes to peer down at her. "I'm thinking about you."

Piper smirked. "Are you though? 'Cause your body is saying one thing and then your face is saying another. What are you thinking so hard about?"

I chuckled and kissed her on the nose. "I promise it's all you, baby."

"Well then," Piper released my cock and ducked under my arms. She walked backward down the aisle. She pulled her shirt over her head and dropped it on the ground. "Prove it." Before disappearing behind a shelf.

She wants to play huh? We could play.

I followed after her, picking up her shirt as I went. I turned around the shelf she had disappeared behind, half hoping she would be there and the other half hoping not to end the game just yet. When I found her pants on the ground, I wasn't disappointed either way.

"Piper," I called out, picking her jeans up. "You seem to be losing something."

A giggle followed by, "Come find me," was my only response.

I could have found her the old fashion way but I was a vampire and the blood rushing to my cock was telling me to hunt. I inhaled deeply taking in Piper's scent. It was one I couldn't get enough of. When Piper was aroused the whole house knew it and came running. Except for me, until now.

I followed the trail of her scent around another bookshelf and found a pale blue bra hanging from one of the books. I carefully took it off the book and brought it to my face, breathing in her intoxicating scent.

"I'm getting real concerned for you here," I commented as I continued the hunt. "You seem to be losing clothing at an alarming rate. Should I just assume you mean to do so?"

Piper's voice came from close by, low and sultry. "Only if you mean to catch me."

I spun around expecting to see her behind me but the aisle was empty. She must be on the other side of this bookshelf. My lips ticked up in a grin and I hurried to get to the other side before she could leave.

I was too slow. All that remained of Piper were her panties which I stuffed into my pocket. Her scent was stronger now and if I wasn't mistaken she was out of clothing to discard.

Moving around the next corner, I found her lounging on one of the couches in the back of the library. She had a book in her hand and was pretending to read it as I came closer. My eyes took their time as they moved down her body. This wasn't the first time I'd seen Piper nude. However this time was different. This time she was mine.

"Are you just going to stare at me all day?" Piper asked, lowering the book down enough to peer over it. "Or are you going to touch me?"

I growled at her, my upper lip curling up and I almost flashed my fangs at her. I stopped. That's right. I couldn't show her my fangs because she didn't know I was a vampire. Then I remembered this isn't the Piper who knew all our darkest secrets and were okay with it. This woman before me had no idea who or what I was. I couldn't even be myself when making love to her.

"Marcus?" Piper sat up on the couch, the teasing gone from her face. "What's wrong?" When I didn't answer, she walked toward me completely confident in her naked body as she cupped my face. "What is it?"

I peered into her eyes wanting so much to go back to a few minutes ago when everything was fine. They weren't fine. And they wouldn't be fine until this whole ordeal was over. I just couldn't do it. I couldn't pretend that she was the Piper I loved. She looked like her and talked like her but she wasn't the real deal.

"I can't. Not here. Not like this." I pulled away from her hands and dropped her clothes before her before turning on my heel. I didn't bother finding my shirt as I stalked out of the library slamming the door soundly behind me.

What kind of idiot am I?

CHAPTER 19

Piper

AFTER THE EMBARRASSING FIASCO with Marcus in the library, I decided that if I was going to act like an unabashed slut then I probably should get on birth control. God knew I didn't need a little person running around in the muck my life had become.

"Okay, Piper," my doctor began holding my chart. "Have you been sexually active?"

I shook my head. "No. But I plan to be...hence the birth control."

My doctor nodded his head and smiled politely. "Of course, now we'll just need to take a urine sample first." He held out a little cup to me.

"A urine sample? Okay." I hopped off the table and headed toward the bathroom off the side of the room.

"Just place the cup in the little door when you are finished," he explained before walking off.

I closed the bathroom door and pulled my pants down holding the little cup underneath me as I did my business. How degrading was this? But doctor's orders.

In hindsight it was good that Marcus had freaked out and left. I wasn't on anything and I hated to be the one to remember to ask them to wear a condom. In my experience, most men act like wearing a condom was the same as wearing a jacket over their Halloween costume. It just ruined the whole thing.

I wasn't a man so I wouldn't know. Condom or no condom it felt the same to me. Though, I supposed for men it would be a little different. Either way, while I sat there naked in the library, I had a moment of clarity - after I had a moment of confusion and anger about being left naked alone - that it was for the best that we didn't have sex. He was my boss after all. Even if he said he didn't pay my actual check.

However, on the off chance that it happened again I wanted to know for sure that I was prepared. So here I was peeing into a little cup at the doctor's office.

Sighing, I put the cup where I had been told and flushed the toilet, washing my hands quickly before leaving the bathroom. I went back to the examination room and sat on the table, waiting for the doctor to appear again.

It didn't take very long before the doctor returned. This time with a curious look on his face.

"Piper," he said.

"Yes?" I answered back, a weird feeling in my gut.

"You said you weren't sexually active?" He held his clipboard to his chest as he stared at me, like I might have been lying.

I stared right back at him. "No. I haven't had sex in…" I thought about it for a moment before saying, "I'd say at least a year."

The doctor's face grew serious and he approached me, lowering his voice to a soothing tone. "The reason I ask is because you're pregnant and usually in these cases I'd be telling you congratulations, but now I'm wondering if you might need to see someone."

"What?" I blinked at him, shaking my head slightly. "I'm sorry, I must have misheard you. I thought you just said I'm pregnant."

"I did."

"That's...that's impossible. I haven't had sex." I breathed out and then in. My heart beat rose rapidly as I processed the information.

"Now Piper, take a few deep breaths, we don't want you to hyperventilate." He placed his hands on my shoulders and showed me how to breathe. I tried to copy him the best I could but my mind was whirling with all the possibilities of how this could have happened. I didn't remember having sex with anyone and I haven't had any black out drunk nights that I could consider. Hell, the closest I'd come to having sex was with

Marcus yesterday and there's no way in hell that could have happened.

"Do you think perhaps you were drugged?" the doctor asked once I got my breathing under control.

I shook my head rapidly. "No. I don't know. I don't remember. Would I remember?"

"Why don't we take a blood test and see if we can pinpoint how far along you are?" He offered with a reassuring smile. "That might help narrow down when this might have happened."

I bobbed my head in answer but I wasn't really listening, not anymore. Even through the nurse taking my blood I seemed to have gone deaf. The only thing playing over and over in my head was the two words: You're pregnant.

I wasn't some innocent school girl. I knew how this all happened. I've even had my share of pregnancy scares but this was just so out there that I couldn't even begin to imagine how it could be possible. Me? Pregnant?"

"Okay, Piper," the doctor came back, staring down at his little clipboard. "It looks like your hCG levels are quite high so I feel confident in saying you're probably close to the end of your first trimester but we'd need an ultrasound to confirm that." When I didn't answer, he stared at me for a long moment. "Piper, have you felt any symptoms? Nausea. Fatigue. Mood swings?"

I shook my head, swallowing thickly. "No. Not that I know of."

"Well, I can get you down to OBGYN and get you an ultrasound if you like. Then we can go from there. What do you say? Piper?"

I stood from the table and shook my head. "I can't. Not...not today. I'll make an appointment."

"Alright then," the doctor followed me as I left the room before I could get very far away, he took me by the arm. "Do you want me to call someone for you? A friend? A boyfriend? You've had quite a shock and I'm not sure you should be alone right now."

I forced a small smile. "No, I'm fine. I'll talk to someone when I get home. Thank you, doctor."

He released me reluctantly and I hurried away. My mind going a million miles a minute, I couldn't even think of anything other than what was going on in my body right then. How? How? How?

I didn't even realize how I'd gotten home when I pulled the car into the driveway of the Durand manor. Darren was outside fiddling with the garden when I arrived. He took one look at me and rushed to my side.

"Piper…are you alright?" The concern on his face was more than that of a worried coworker. It was almost like we were closer than that.

I chuckled and rubbed my face. "I must look horrible if you're asking me that."

Darren paused and then said, "You are looking rather pale."

"Am I?" I touched my cheeks with both hands and found them cold. Not surprising since I felt like I might just keel over and die at any moment. Then I'd wake up and this had all been a bad dream.

"Maybe you should go lie down." Darren wrapped an arm around my waist and tried to lead me toward the house.

I shrugged him off with a curious look. "It's okay. I can walk. Thanks."

A flash of hurt went across Daren's face for a second and then it was gone. "Oh, okay. Sorry."

This day just got weirder and weirder.

I walked in the back door and into the kitchen where Gretchen stood behind the stove.

"Oh, Piper," she greeted with a smile and then frowned at me. "You're looking sick. Are you alright? Want me to make you some soup?"

I shook my head. "No, thanks. I'm okay. I might come get something later."

"Okay..." Gretchen replied, her eyes following me as I walked up the stairs.

Unfortunately, I wasn't able to get to my room right away to have a mental breakdown. Rayne was waiting for me by my bedroom door.

"Hey, no offense but I'm not feeling too hot right now. Can we talk later?" I told him as soon as I was near.

Rayne pursed his lips and looked me over. Without asking he touched my forehead and then frowned. "You don't have a fever. Maybe you have a bug?"

Yeah a bug called pregnancy!

"You're what now?"

I frowned. "Huh?"

"I mean," Rayne cleared his throat and shifted in place. "Do you think you might have a bug?"

I swallowed and nodded trying my best not to burst into tears. "Yeah, I'm sure that's all it is." I grabbed my door handle and turned it. "I'm just going to go to bed for now."

"Alright, I'll check on you later." Then Rayne was gone before I could even say thank you.

CHAPTER 20
Rayne

THE MOMENT PIPER TURNED her back I dashed away. If I had a heart it would be running a mile a minute. As it were it took less than a dozen heart beats to get from the upstairs to barreling down the basement stairs.

When I came barging in, everyone in the room jumped to their feet in alert ready to fight whatever was coming our way. Thankfully, Antoine for once was downstairs and not in his office. I didn't want to have to repeat this.

"What is it Rayne? What's the commotion?" Wynn asked from this bed, placing the book he had in his hand on the side table.

If I had to breathe I would have been out of breath from running so quickly down there. In fact, I wished I did breathe so that I had a moment to collect my thoughts. Cause honestly I wasn't even sure I knew what the hell I was going to say.

"Just spit it out already," Drake said, leaning against the back of the couch.

"Piper," I got out, my eyes darting to each of my brothers in turn. "Piper's pregnant."

The entire room went still. Not the kind that happens with humans where you can hear the heart beats still. Vampires were different. We didn't have to move or breathe any of those little twitches that humans had. We did them because it made us less alarming to others. To be perfectly still as the dead like right now was a gift only vampires had.

"Well?" I spun around in a circle, searching for some kind of reaction. "Piper's pregnant. Someone say something!" I grabbed the sides of my hair, pulling at them frantically.

Antoine walked up beside me, placing a hand on my shoulder. "Are you sure?"

I shrugged his hand off. "What do you mean, am I sure? I just heard it from the source's mind. Piper is one hundred percent pregnant."

"Maybe you heard wrong?" Allister moved away from his bed toward me. "Maybe she was thinking of something else?"

I shook my head, anger welling up inside me. "I didn't mistake this. Plus you didn't see the way she looked when she got home. She looked like she saw a ghost."

Drake snorted. "Well, I would too if I was pregnant out of the blue. I mean, Piper doesn't know she's had loads of sex, like I mean a whole lot of sex in the last month alone. She probably thinks she's going crazy."

"Or worse," Allister said quietly.

Crap. I hadn't thought about that.

Turning to Antoine, I begged, "We have to fix this. We have to explain it to her. We can't let her think she was…" I swallowed hard, unable to make myself say it.

"Violated," Wynn supplied for me.

I nodded.

Antoine followed my sentiment and turned away for a moment before turning back to me. "You are sure this is what you heard?"

"I wouldn't lie about this." I shook my head and then sighed. "I try to stay out of her head for the most part but she seemed really off when I was waiting for her to get home from her…" I paused and looked around the room. "Does anyone know where she went?"

"I believe she went to a doctor's appointment," Marcus provided, staring down at his hands.

I angled my head to the side. "Why would you know that?"

"I heard her telling Darren this morning."

Frowning, I pushed at Marcus's head, searching for answers. I saw a flash of Piper's nude body and knew what had happened. "You and Piper almost banged in the library?"

"Ah, you sly dog you." Drake chuckled, clapping Marcus on the shoulder. "And in the library? Couldn't use one of the dozens of beds in the house huh?"

Marcus pushed away from Drake. "Nothing happened." We all stared at him expectantly. "I stopped it before anything could happen. I didn't want her to..." he sighed and shook his head sadly. "It's not the same."

"I get it," I told him, giving him a sympathetic smile. "She's Piper but not our Piper. I think I'd have a hard time doing it too with this version of her."

"Can you hear what she's thinking now?" Allister asked, staring up at the ceiling.

I angled my head though it wasn't really an ear thing, more of an inside my head thing and focused on Piper.

"She's screaming into her pillow right now," Marcus explained. "It's faint but it's there."

"She must be so scared and confused right now," Wynn murmured and I felt his sadness. I wanted to be there for Piper as well.

"So what are we going to do?" I turned to Antoine. "This obviously isn't going away and she's going to figure it out eventually.

Wouldn't it be best to take her back to the council and have them undo what they did?"

Antoine rubbed his forehead and stared down at the ground. "To have them undo this would put us right back in the position we were before."

"I don't care." Allister jumped in and we all looked to him. "I mean, if it means I'm on trial for murder again. I don't care. I won't let Piper suffer this alone. I love her more than that."

"As do we all, Allister," Antoine countered, tucking his hands into his pockets. "But we can't just march in there making demands. "We first need to find out how far along she is and then we can move on from there."

"What does it matter how far along she is?" Drake demanded, getting into Antoine's face. "She already knows she's pregnant."

Antoine didn't let Drake push him around. "If she's only at the beginning then it might be possible for Rayne to make her forget the last few hours and we can continue on as before. She won't start showing for a while and the symptoms can easily be passed off as a sickness."

Drake scoffed. "I can't believe you are saying this. You want to let her forget she knows she's pregnant and just go back to business as usual."

"I know it sounds heartless, Draconius. But if the hunters find out she's pregnant there could be repercussions. Ones we don't want to deal with."

"Like what?" Allister asked sincerely. "What would they do?"

Antoine shrugged a shoulder. "They may decide that Piper is too valuable to lose. OR they may decide they want the baby for themselves. Can you imagine what they could do with a baby that's half human half vampire? Or what if it's all human servant? It would be twice as powerful as any of us and used as a killing machine."

"I won't let that happen," Drake announced.

"Neither will I," Marcus moved in closer to the group.

I groaned. "I guess it's up to me to find out how far along she is huh?"

Drake smirked, bumping me on the shoulder. "Well you are the only one with the inside scoop."

My head drooped, letting my hair fall over my face. "Fine. I'll go snoop. But I'm still not sure this is such a good idea."

CHAPTER 21
Piper

MY EYES BURNED. PROBABLY from all the crying I'd been doing. My life was over and I didn't even remember how. I mean if I'm going to get knocked up I want to damn sure have the memory of that night in my brain.

Unless it's not a pleasant one and then I want nothing to do with it.

The major problem now was whether or not I was going to keep it.

I placed a hand on my stomach and stared down at it. "What should I do?"

As if the baby could answer me back. I sighed. I needed someone to talk to about this. I couldn't call my mother because she'd just give me crap about ruining my life like I'd ruined her. Or she'd ask me for money. My dad was out of the picture too.

A knock on my door pulled me from my thoughts. "Piper? It's Gretchen. I brought you some soup."

Oh. Gretchen. Now there's a kindly face that might lend me an ear.

I hopped out of bed and rushed for the door. Throwing it open, I smiled at the older woman. "Thank God you're here."

Gretchen walked in with a tray and sat it on the table. She lifted the lid off the soup and steam came out with all the soupy goodness. The smell of the soup should have made me hungry but all I felt was nauseated.

I covered my mouth and turned away. "Oh my God get that out of here." I plugged my nose and waved behind me. "Please just cover it back up. Now."

Gretchen hurried to do what I asked but not fast enough. I couldn't stop it and ran for the bathroom. While I hurled my guts out I questioned my life choices.

How had I gotten here? Did someone have it out to get me? I thought I was doing alright. I had finally gotten a new job. I wasn't living in my car. There was even a guy I liked.

Fuck. Marcus. How was I going to tell him about this?

Gretchen calmly walked in and wet a washcloth in the sink. She knelt beside me by the toilet and patted my forehead with the clothes and then sat it on the back of my neck.

"Thanks," I said weakly, smiling at her.

Gretchen sat down on the edge of the tub and asked, "How far along are you?"

My head jerked up. "What?"

She smiled and chuckled. "You don't think I don't know morning sickness when I see it?"

I sank down further onto the floor, staring at the bathroom tile. "The doctor says about three months. Maybe more, maybe less. They'd have to do an ultrasound."

Gretchen patted my back. "Well, don't worry. We'll take good care of you."

My brows furrowed, I stared up at her. "You're not going to ask me who the father is?"

She shrugged a shoulder. "Not my place. I see someone in need and I help them. Simple as that." Gretchen stood and offered me her hands. "Now let's get you to bed. I'll bring you some crackers and ginger ale for morning sickness. You let me know if you feel up to eating anything. Anything at all." She explained as she helped me lay down. "I'll make sure you get taken care of."

I returned her smile, finally not feeling completely out of my mind with worry since I found out I was pregnant. Maybe it would be alright?

So what if it didn't know who the father was? Lots of women didn't know. I'd be fine. I'd be fine.

I kept repeating that to myself hoping that it would make me believe it and I fell asleep.

I must have dozed for a while because when I woke up it was evening. Turning toward my night stand, I found crackers and ginger ale waiting for me.

Picking up one of the crackers, I nibbled on it as I walked toward the bedroom door.

Now that my nausea had subsided I found myself starving.

I made my way to the kitchen through the backstairs. I jerked to a stop when I heard raised voices.

"What do you mean you're just going to wait and see?" Darren shouted in a tone I'd never heard from him before.

"I'm saying that we don't know how far along she is," Antoine answered back with an impatient sigh.

"Gretchen said that the doctor told Piper she was about three months along. I don't think your wait and see approach is going to work." Darren kept going, confusing me more and more by the second. "What are you going to do when she wakes up one morning and she's got a huge belly? You can't just wipe her memories and make her pretend it's not there. That's not going to work."

"Obviously not," Antoine answered. There was a pause before Antoine continued, "Have you taken a moment to consider this may be your child?"

I gasped. My hand went to my mouth to stifle the sound. It was too late.

"Piper?" Antoine called up the stairs. "Is that you?"

Forcing myself not to freak out, I stiffly walked down the stairs and faced the two of them. Three of them I guess since Marcus was in the corner with his arms over his chest not saying anything.

"Someone better start talking because I'm this close from calling the cops," I croaked out, the tears and angry frustration coming to the surface.

"Piper," Darren began, moving toward me.

"No, don't touch me. You did this to me. Didn't you?" I couldn't help it as my voice rose to a shrill pitch. "What did you do, drug me? Why can't I remember it? Or you? Why are you all looking at me like I'm something that needs to be coddled and protected."

I didn't give them a chance to answer as I shoved between them to get to the fridge. "And another thing. Why do you rarely eat anything but what's in these?" I held up the container and took a drink. I quickly spit it out as the cold copper taste hit my tongue. "Blood?" I stared at Darren and threw the container, splattering the red liquid across the wall. "You told me the last maid was into some weird vampire stuff, not the rest of you too!"

"Piper," Marcus tried to grab for me. "Please calm down."

"No!" I jerked away from him. "You calm down. I want answers. What kind of freak show is this?"

"Piper. Calm down." There was something different about Antoine's voice. Something about it made me want to do what he said.

I fought against it not wanting to remain calm. I just knew that if I stayed calm something bad was going to happen to me.

"She's fighting my control," Antoine said strangely. "She doesn't even have her abilities and she's able to fight back against me."

I locked my eyes on him and glared. "Let me go!"

Something snapped and I was finally able to feel the full force of my emotions again. This time I didn't wait around for answers.

I ran.

The doorbell rang as I clambered through the dining room and toward the front. I could feel them behind me, closing in as if I were a prey to their predator.

Before any of them could grab me, I swung open the front door. A man dressed like some eighties mobster stood on the doorstep. He took one look at me and grinned.

"Piper! I'm so happy to see you're doing better," he exclaimed, moving into the house without asking. "When Antoine told me you were sick I was beside myself with worry. But lucky for me to stop by again and run into you."

I stared at the man having no idea who he was whatsoever. "Antoine told you I was sick?"

The man in question walked into the room, Marcus and Darren coming up behind him. My world came crashing down on me as I realized something. Maybe I was sick? Maybe I didn't remember getting pregnant because something really bad happened to me and my mind is helping me not to remember.

Or maybe it's all a lot of horse shit and nobody was telling the truth.

"It's not," Rayne said, coming down the front stairs. "It's not horse shit."

I gaped at him. "Did you just read my mind?"

Rayne nodded. "Yes."

This was unbelievable. These people are crazy. I had to get out of here. Maybe this guy could help.

"Vincent is not the one to turn to," Rayne said before I could even open my mouth. "We'll explain everything if you just calm down."

"I'm sorry," Vincent stepped in with a frown. "I seem to have wandered in on something. Is this a bad time?"

"No," I quickly said as the others said in unison, "Yes."

"Ah, I see." Vincent turned to me scanning my form for something before saying, "I'm not sure what's going on here but if you're going to honor our agreement I won't wait forever. I expect to have an answer soon."

"An answer to what?" I asked, baffled by what he was saying.

Vincent, as he was called, twisted a ring on his finger and frowned. "To the location of the vampire council, of course. Are you alright? It's almost like you don't want your freedom from the hunters. Or have you changed your mind?"

"Huh?" I blinked at him not computing the words that just came out of his mouth.

Vincent stepped closer to me. "You know if you're not happy here with these blood suckers. We hunters would be happy to have you."

Blood suckered? Hunters? What in the world?

Then it clicked.

The leather outfits. The lingerie. The vials of blood hidden all over my room. The way the Durands seemed to act so casually around me as if I were some lowly servant. This was all real. This was my life. It wasn't some supernatural fantasy. These guys were vampires and if I understood right the man walking out the door was a vampire hunter. So what was I doing with either of them?

"Just think about it would you?" Vincent said from the door and I almost called out to him. Almost asked him to get me away from these strangers. But something inside me stopped me.

Maybe it was some emotion I forgot or maybe it was my need to know how I ended up pregnant and missing a significant part of my memory. All I knew was that the only place I was going to get answers from was here and I couldn't run away. Not now.

"Are you ready Piper?" Rayne asked, holding out his hand to me. "Are you ready to find out the truth?"

I swallowed down the bile rising, my eyes darting between the others then back to the hand offered to me.

Sliding my hand into his, I licked my lips and said, "I'm ready."

CHAPTER 22

Piper

MY STOMACH KNOTTED AROUND itself the whole drive. I still wasn't sure I'd made the right decision but getting my memories back was more important than anything. I could figure out the rest later.

"Do not worry, pet. Everything will be fine." Wynn tried to hold my hand and I jerked away, moving as far away from him as I could. The hurt in his eyes made my chest ache but I shoved it down.

There was no way that I was dating these guys. Vampires. Monsters. Or whatever they were. All I knew was that what I saw in the park wasn't human.

I was human. I knew I was. I ate. I slept. I shit. I had a heart beat. I had nausea. Oh God. Is this ever going to stop?

My hand rested on my stomach. I had a life inside of me and I didn't even know which one of them was the father. My eyes tried to look around the limo but I forced them back out the window.

Was it even any of their baby? Could vampires have babies? What if it came out with little fangs? What if it tried to eat its way out of my stomach like in that alien movie?

"Piper," Rayne said.

I jerked at my name. "What?"

"That's not going to happen." The sympathy in Rayne's eyes only pissed me off.

I scowled at him. "Stay out of my head!"

"I'm just saying," Rayne continued completely unfazed by me. "You're being irrational. Nothing like that is going to happen."

I crossed my arms over my chest and muttered, "How do you know?"

Wynn answered. "Because vampire babies are highly unlikely. The older the vampire, the less active his..." He waved a hand in front of him as if trying to think of the word. "...seed."

"So you're saying your sperm is as dead as you are," I snapped.

Giving an elegant nonchalant shrug, Wynn said, "More or less."

"What he means," Drake interjected, "is that all of us over a hundred years old are dried up. Poof." He opened his hands in front of him like an explosion was happening. "Nothing but shooting blanks there, honey."

"Don't call me that," I growled and then glanced around the limo before my eyes landed on Darren's head in the front seat. "So you're telling me that Darren, the only other human of the bunch, is the only likely father?"

Darren's eyes met mine through the rear view mirror for an instant.

"Not exactly," Drake continued. "While the rest of us are well past our peak," he clamped his hand on Rayne's leg. "Rayne here is barely sixty. He could have just as likely knocked you up."

Rayne shoved Drake's hand off his knee. "Thanks but don't help me."

"No, no," I stopped him from cutting Drake off more. "I should know who the father of my offspring is going to be. I mean since apparently I've been slutting it up with the whole lot of you."

Allister lifted his hand.

I sighed. "What?"

"I wouldn't call it that. We all have a genuine relationship with you that we cherish. To label it as something as simple as sex is an offense to our whole dynamic."

I snorted. "Well, I'm sorry if it's a little hard to believe I fell for all of you."

Allister raised his hand again.

"Oh my fucking God if you raise your hand again I will cut it off and feed it to you! Just say what you want to say." I couldn't even believe what I was saying. Had I ever been this blood thirsty? I don't think I'd ever threatened anyone in my entire life. Maybe they do know me better than I know myself.

The idea was frightening and a little thrilling.

Drake chuckled. "That's the Piper we all know and love."

"Actually," Allister interrupted. "What I was going to say was that you haven't slept with all of us. You and Marcus as far as I know, have yet to consummate your feelings for one another."

While Drake burst out laughing making fun of his brother for the way he worded things, I stared at Marcus.

My mind went back to that day in the library where Marcus had me pressed up against the wall, his fingers doing all kinds of naughty delicious things to my nether regions. Then he stopped. Almost as if he had thought of somewhere else to be.

I did remember being confused because he'd said, "Not like this. Not now."

At the time, I thought he meant not in the library. Maybe it was something else.

"You had a chance to and you didn't..." I watched his face as I asked the question, "Why?"

Marcus' eyes did not waver from mine as he answered. "I want you as you truly are. As the woman we all love. Not for some cheap trick to appease the council."

"Aww," Drake smacked Marcus on the shoulder. "Look at that, you do know how to woo a woman."

Marcus shot Drake a murderous look that I matched.

"Everyone," Darren called out. "We're here."

Antoine, who had been quite for the ride, spoke now. "Let me do the talking. We do not know how the council will react to the news. They won't be happy to have their game cut short. So it's just best if we all remain calm and explain the situation."

The others muttered their agreement while my insides rolled. More vampires. More bloodshed. I didn't know if I could handle it.

"Piper?" Antoine asked, offering me his hand. "Are you ready?"

I placed my hand in Antoine's, allowing him to help me out of the limo.

We walked up to a club with a large neon sign and big bold blood red letters, reading Club Dead. I could only imagine what was inside the club with the name like Club Dead, it probably was a club for monsters just like everything else I'd come across lately.

Antoine didn't let go of my hand as we walked to the club entrance. It was not like any club I'd ever been in. It wasn't loud and boisterous with people lining up to get in. There were only the two large guards that seemed to have as much personality as a wooden stick.

Once inside, we walked down a long hallway, the lights dimmed, but no music playing.

I felt like we were marching to our deaths and every single step made my stomach knot tighter and tighter.

Antoine squeezed my hand.

I knew he was trying to be reassuring, only it wasn't.

Maybe if I had my memories, I'd be okay with this. Maybe if I knew what the hell was going on. I wouldn't feel like I was ready to throw up all over the floor. However, that also could just be my morning sickness talking.

Finally, we arrived in the main part of the club.

We walked by a bar that had a single bartender standing behind it. There was no one else in the club, the couches and the chairs all empty. The lights, thrown on, even though no one was there to care. The bartender didn't even bother glancing up at us as we walked into the room.

When we approached the couches Antoine paused, and told me to sit down. I did as he asked even though the rest of them stood around me.

Rayne walked over to the bartender, having a low conversation with him, that I couldn't hear.

"Don't worry so much Piper," Drake told me. "We'll take care of you. We won't let anything happen to you. Remember, we're on your side."

Knowing what I knew, I wasn't sure it was very comforting.

We sat there for a few minutes, twiddling our thumbs, not bothering to talk between ourselves. I wondered if the guys were as nervous as I was. Or if they knew something I didn't and, most likely, they were biding their time for something to happen, something that they didn't want to tell me.

After a few minutes passed, the clacking of shoes on the tile floor alerted me to someone approaching.

I glanced toward the sound and saw a little girl. No more than eight or nine in a tea length dress all ruffled and billowing around her, her curls were pulled up in a pretty little bow. She looked completely out of place in the club.

She smiled when she saw me and rushed to my side. "Piper," she exclaimed. "I'm so happy to see you. I didn't expect you to be back so soon."

I glanced down at the little girl who held onto my arm, hugging it tightly like we were old friends. For all I knew, we might be.

I patted on the back of her head, letting out an awkward, "Hello."

"Oh, right." The girl pulled away from me with a frown. "You don't know who I am. I'm Odette."

"Hello, Odette." I offered her a small smile." It's nice to meet you. But it seems like you have me at a disadvantage." Pursing my lips, I stared down at the girl. I wasn't sure if it was my maternal instincts kicking in or just the sight of the little girl surrounded by vampires I didn't like. "What are you doing here? Where are your parents?"

"Piper," Allister placed his hand on my shoulder. "Odette is one of the council members."

I stared down at the child in confusion.

One of the council members. How could a child be a council member?

Odette flashed me a pretty smile, fangs and all.

"Ah, Antoine!" A dark skinned man walked into the room followed by another man of no unique description. "What do we owe the pleasure of your company this evening?"

"You have to fix me." I jumped up from my seat knowing I was going against everything Antoine had instructed. "Give my memories back now."

"Tuma, my apologies." Antoine intercepted and then turned to me. "Piper," Antoine warned, placing his hands on my shoulders. "What did we discuss?"

I shook him off. "I don't care what we discussed. I want to know what's going on and I want to know now."

"Oh my," Tuma tut-tutted. "This is quite a development. Not even a week out and already you're quitting?" He glanced over at his companion. "Is this why you suggested this game? You knew they'd fail so fast?"

The man shook his head. "No. I knew they'd fail but not for the reason they're here."

I stepped back. The way the man was staring at me made me suddenly uneasy. "What does it matter why we're here? Just give them back."

"Now, now Miss Piper," Tuma pursed his lips and stepped up to me, his golden cane pointed toward me. "Memories or not, you shouldn't be rude to strangers. You never know what they might do." He let his fangs peek between his lips.

I growled. "Look, no offense but I just found out I had my memories tampered with, I work for vampires and I'm banging most of them." I gestured back to the group and then let out a bitter laugh. "And to top off this stack of crazy, I'm pregnant! And I don't even know who the father is or if he's human or vampire. So excuse me if I left the niceties at the door."

"Oh my. That is quite a conundrum." Tuma looked me over and then to his friend.

"Did you not see this before we issued out our punishment, Caleb?"

The man, Caleb, shook his head. "No. The Piper before had no knowledge of her pregnancy and I couldn't read any signs of another inside of her."

"A baby!" Odette squealed racing to my side to clutch me around the waist. "I'm so excited! You must stay here and let us take care of you."

"Uh..." I stared down at the little girl still having an issue thinking of her as a blood sucking fiend. "I'm not sure that's a good idea. Why don't we worry about that after I get my memories back?"

"Yes, yes," Tuma agreed with me. "My apologies, Miss Piper. If we had known we would have found a more fitting punishment. No one likes to upset pregnant women. We don't want to risk hurting the baby."

Frowning, I scanned the three council members' faces. "So you don't care that I might be pregnant with a vampire?"

"Of course not! We're delighted," Tuma explained. "Whether it be a human offspring or that of a vampire. Either way, a child of a human servant is special and should be treated as such." He gestured to Caleb with his two fingers. "Now Caleb, give this dear woman her memories back before she goes into premature labor from all the shock."

Odette stepped away from me as Caleb came forward. I stared at the quiet man, my heart racing as he reached his hand out. Shooting a look behind me, the Durands weren't at all concerned about what was about to happen. This made me relax slightly but not enough to keep me from flinching when Caleb's hand touched my forehead.

"This shouldn't take long," he said right before I was overrun with images.

Images poured into my head, blinding me to everything before me. My heart beat hard enough that I swore it was going to jump out of my chest. The insides of my head were so full of voices and feelings that I wouldn't have been surprised had it exploded all over the floor just like Morpheus's had a few days earlier.

Then all of my senses came back at once. The air was thicker. The ground beneath my feet was more firm. I could actually taste the air as I inhaled. Then there was a heart beat but it wasn't mine. I focused on that sound, reaching down inside of me until I found it.

There.

That's my baby.

Oh my God. That's my baby!

My eyes flipped open and I stared around the room, my mouth open wide as I searched for the guys. My guys.

"I'm going to have a baby," I gasped, and then grinned at them. "We're going to have a baby!"

The others grinned back at me with as much enthusiasm as I had, if not more. I noticed Darren hadn't come in with us but figured I had plenty of time to jump around with him later. Once I got away from the crazies.

Speaking of crazies...

I turned from the guys and said again a bit more slowly, "I'm going to have a baby." I slapped my forehead and sank into a nearby chair, Caleb moving back to his spot. "What the hell am I going to do?"

"I'm not sure what you mean," Tuma asked, stopping before me. "A baby is a joyous thing. Especially one as special as yours. It has to be protected."

"The hunters," I said quickly, turning my eyes up to Antoine. "If they find out I'm pregnant. Especially if it's a superhuman baby, I just know that asshole Vincent will find somewhere to use it."

"Do not worry, Piper." Antoine came toward me with a confident stride. "No one will hurt our baby."

"That's right," Tuma interjected, stepping too close for comfort. "And to make sure you do not fall into the wrong hands I believe it would be best if you stayed with us."

"Now hold on a minute," Drake argued.

Antoine held his hand up. Drake backed off, but just barely.

"Is this a new form of punishment, Tuma? Because I will not let you or anyone else have our baby." The deadly tone in Antoine's voice made me shiver.

Tuma gasped, placing a hand on his chest. "I am offended you would think so little of us. Do you think we would really harm such an innocent thing?"

When the Durands only stared at him, Tuma sighed. "Very well, I swear a blood oath that none of the council members or any of our own will harm your child or the child's mother until after she has been placed back into your protection." He bit into his hand and let the blood flow onto the floor before him.

Odette came over to me and grabbed my hands. "Come on, I'll show you where you will stay."

I stared at Antoine for a moment wondering if this was really happening. I'd been so happy a few minutes ago and once again my life was in danger and not just mine but that of my child. Did I really have a choice in the matter?

The hunters or the council. Now where had I heard that one before?

"Don't worry," Odette held my hand tightly. "I love babies. They're so soft and adorable." She giggled in that high pitched voice of hers and added, "Plus, they taste good too!"

I forced a smile back down at her, while on the inside screaming, "Someone get me the fuck out of here!!"

About the Author

Erin Bedford is an otaku, recovering coffee addict, and Legend of Zelda fanatic. Her brain is so full of stories that need to be told that she must get them out or explode into a million screaming chibis. Obsessed with fairy tales and bad boys, she hasn't found a story she can't twist to match her deviant mind full of innuendos, snarky humor, and dream guys.

On the outside, she's a work from home mom and bookbinger. One the inside, she's a thirteen-year-old boy screaming to get out and tell you the pervy joke they found online. As an ex-computer programmer, she dreams of one day combining her love for writing and college credits to make the ultimate video game!

Until then, when she's not writing, Erin is devouring as many books as possible on her quest to have the biggest book gut of all time. She's written over thirty books, ranging from paranormal romance, urban fantasy, and even scifi romance.